S0-AXB-874

Savage Desert

Center Point
Large Print

Also by Lewis B. Patten and available from
Center Point Large Print:

Outlaw Canyon
Wild Waymire

**This Large Print Book carries the
Seal of Approval of N.A.V.H.**

Savage Desert

A Western Duo

Lewis B. Patten

CENTER POINT LARGE PRINT
THORNDIKE, MAINE

This Center Point Large Print edition is published
in the year 2014 in conjunction with
Golden West Literary Agency.

The text of this Large Print edition is unabridged.
In other aspects, this book may vary
from the original edition.
Printed in the United States of America
on permanent paper.
Set in 16-point Times New Roman type.

ISBN: 978-1-61173-966-4

Library of Congress Cataloging-in-Publication Data

Patten, Lewis B.
 Savage Desert : A Western Duo / Lewis B. Patten. — Center Point
Large Print edition.
 pages cm
 ISBN 978-1-61173-966-4 (Library binding : alk. paper)
 1. Large type books. I. Title.
 PS3566.A79S287 2014
 813′.54—dc23
                                                        2013033443

Savage Desert

Table of Contents

★ ★ ★ ★ ★

The Killer in Him

★ ★ ★ ★ ★

I

At 5:00 p.m., the first flake struck Johnny McNaul's freckled nose. It was a big one, but it melted as soon as it touched his skin. He looked up then, to watch the wall of snow roll down the valley. In the distance the snow was gray and dirty, obscuring the meadows at the head of the valley and the huge, flat face of rimrock that wore its fringe of dark blue spruce like a crown.

With a boy's wonder, Johnny stood still, rapt face uptilted to the storm, and let it roll over him. The full fury of the cottony flakes enveloped him and he laughed. He stuck his tongue out, feeling the sharp, sweet moisture as the snow melted, and watching his steaming breath.

Quickly his coat was covered, and now a new fascination gripped him. Far from being anonymous blobs of white, each flake had a beauty of its own, star-shaped, an endless variety of pattern with never two alike. . . .

The bellow of Ross McNaul's voice broke into his thoughts, beating muffled through the storm: "Johnny! Hey, Johnny! Come on in here!"

Johnny made his shuffling and reluctant way through the blinding and unreal world of whirling white, coming shortly to the one-room house with its gray and solid log walls, its long low verandah.

Ross McNaul stood before the door, big, square,

and dependable, his mouth making its usual long and somber line across his spare and dark-tanned face. Ross's eyes were bright bits of pale blue sky, and now they showed the only expression in Ross's face, a smiling and half-amused friendliness. Ross said: "Some storm, eh? Man could get lost a hundred yards from the house."

There was never much show of affection between these two, yet affection was there, deep and unspoken, a harmony of thought and action that showed itself only in the quiet respect each had for the desires and utterances of the other.

Up the valley, beyond the big, vacant owner's house, cattle began to bawl, these sudden, uneasy sounds making a chorus that seemed to have no direction, that seemed to hang disembodied behind this curtain of storm. Down by the bunkhouse a door slammed, and Ross McNaul put his bellow in that direction: "Sikes! If you an' Joe got anything laying around on the ground, better pick it up, or you won't find it again till spring!"

A horse materialized startlingly before them, rider and horse both being nearly invisible for the coat of white they wore, and the voice of Ernest Pfarr struck heavily at them: "Ross, ain't this a heller?"

There had been a sort of magic in the sudden onslaught of storm. Suddenly it was gone, and in its place was the uneasiness and the fear that invariably came when Pfarr came. Pfarr was Circle Dot's foreman, a slight man with hair turned prematurely white, a man whose face was lined with age and weather. Briefly Johnny wondered why it was that the lines that time developed in a man's face could be so different in different men. Sikes, one of Circle Dot's year-around cowpunchers, had a face as seamed as that of Pfarr, yet the lines in Sikes's face bespoke only kindliness and humor, showing none of the scheming wickedness so apparent in Pfarr.

Ross McNaul said shortly—"Johnny, go shut the door to the chicken house."—completing with his tone and his sharp withdrawal, the uneasy discomfort that Pfarr had begun by his appearance.

Johnny slouched off, hearing as he went Ross's unfriendly: "I thought you were down on the desert for the winter. You sure picked a devil of a time to show up here."

And Pfarr's sibilant, insinuating: "So you know she's coming? You want the inside track. Quit thinking about it, Ross. She'd have no truck with a blamed. . . ."

Ross's voice laid itself on Pfarr like a whip. "Shut up!"

Knowing this was wrong, Johnny halted ten yards away, completely hidden by the snow, yet close enough to hear each word. Ross's voice turned low, full of anger, yet with a controlled

13

quality about it, a caution that puzzled Johnny. Ross said: "I've warned you before, and I'll warn you again. If Johnny ever finds out, I'll kill you."

Pfarr's raspy voice fawned: "Ross, you know me better than that. He won't find out from me. You've played along like a sensible man and it's been profitable for us both. Why would I spoil it?"

Ross's tone lost none of its unfriendliness. "Who's coming?"

"Don't play dumb, Ross. Judith Connors. Who else?"

"What the devil for? It's winter. Why would she come here when she could stay in New York and be comfortable?"

"Connors is dead. Maybe she wants to be sure we're taking good care of her cattle." Pfarr laughed, but there was no mirth in his laugh. "We're doing that, ain't we, Ross? We're taking damned good care of her cattle."

Ross McNaul's voice was low, hardly distinguishable to Johnny, but its quality was intense and bitter. "Damn you, Pfarr. Damn you. If it wasn't for Johnny, I'd. . . ."

Pfarr's reply was freighted with threat and ugliness. "No you wouldn't, Ross. You haven't got the guts. And stay away from Judith Connors, you hear? She's likely as scrawny as an old gummer cow, but if there's any marryin' to be done, I'll do it."

Johnny heard his father's futile, enraged snort, heard the house door open and slam. A square of light showed dimly against the wall of swirling white that separated Johnny from the house.

Suddenly Johnny was frightened. Complete depression of mind and body settled down over him. *I wish he'd go away an' leave us alone!* he said to himself.

Always it was this way when Ernest Pfarr put in one of his infrequent appearances at Circle Dot. Johnny's father became surly and short-tempered, remained so for a week after Pfarr had gone. Johnny knew it would be worse this time, for this time there would be no escape into the outdoors for Johnny.

Feeling his way carefully through snow already three inches deep, Johnny reached the hen house and slammed the door, dropping a bolt down through the hasp to secure it.

As he made his way back toward the house, the air took on a sudden sharpness, a bitter cold that had not been there before. Cattle drifted through the yard, heads lowered, snow a cover on their backs, their tails wind-whipped between their legs.

Johnny came into the house with the brief statement, "Cattle's driftin', Pa."

"Sure." Ross's voice lacked its usual easy friendliness. "They'll drift till they find shelter. Storm'll be over in the morning."

Ernest Pfarr attempted joviality: "How you gettin' along, boy?"

Johnny thought—*All right, till you came.*—but he said: "All right, Mister Pfarr. All right, I guess."

There might have been pleasure in this howling night of storm, snug and secure behind four log walls. There might have been pleasure but for Ernest Pfarr. Instead, there was only silence, supper in silence and afterward only the howl of the storm and the even snores of Ernest Pfarr. Afterward only the wakeful restless tossing of Ross McNaul in the bed beside Johnny.

Johnny was nine, old enough to know that Ernest Pfarr held some secret knowledge of his own as a threat over Ross's head, old enough to know when big Ross McNaul was afraid. . . .

Dawn, instead of bringing surcease from the storm, brought an intensification. In the yard at Circle Dot, snow made a cover over the ground eighteen inches deep, and still it came, sifting from an apparently endless supply in the deep-gray clouds above.

Johnny McNaul's particular chores included feeding the chickens, gathering of eggs, carrying in wood that this morning had to be dug out of the snow, and milking Circle Dot's single milch cow.

As he made his rounds, plowing through the deep snow, he let his mind dwell idly on his father, on Ernest Pfarr, on the coming of Judith Connors, who he had never seen.

Ernest Pfarr was foreman of Circle Dot, but made of it a part-time job, being away from the ranch a good part of the time. In his absence, Ross McNaul was ramrod. In summer, Circle Dot employed as many as a dozen cowpunchers, but in winter this crew was cut to two or three. Circle Dot put up only enough hay in summer for the saddle stock and for the milch cow. The cattle roamed the hillsides, the valley meadows, finding always enough forage to carry them through the winter in this land of open winters, of almost daily sunshine.

This morning, however, the cattle stood dumbly the length of the valley, rumps to the storm, heads hanging dispiritedly. Johnny pitied them briefly and went into the house, stamping his feet and breathing hard from exertion.

That he had interrupted something was obvious from the sudden and uneasy silence, from the self-consciously downcast eyes of his father.

It is the way of a boy to forget trouble quickly. Out in the snow this morning, he had all but forgotten the trouble of last night, but now it was revived, for he knew that while he had been gone the same conversation of last night had been renewed. Silently he took his place at the rude table.

At some time in his past, Ross McNaul had done

something of which he was ashamed, or afraid. Ernest Pfarr knew of it, used his knowledge to force something from Ross McNaul. But what was the thing he was forcing from Ross?

Pfarr spoke then, in his falsely hearty voice: "If she don't come today, she'll play hell getting here. This weather ain't going to quit."

Johnny asked: "How'll she come, Pa? Horse-back?"

Ross shook his head. "Not her. She'll come by train to Antelope, down on the desert. Stage upriver sixty miles to Wild Horse. She'll have to hire a rig there to bring her up to the ranch. If it keeps snowing, she'll maybe have to come horseback from Wild Horse."

Johnny said: "Gee, an' it ain't ten miles to Antelope over the mountain."

"Rough, though. Too rough for a woman. Besides, you got to know the trails. You'd never get a woman to come down through the rim when there's eighteen inches of snow on the trail."

Pfarr snorted. "Blame foolishness. With all her money, I can't see why she'd come here at all . . . especially in winter."

Johnny looked at him. Ernest Pfarr stood beside the table, his seamed face smiling, but with something wholly and habitually evil even in his smile.

He stood but shoulder high to big Ross McNaul, was wizened and slightly stooped. His gun belt sagged from the weight of the big Colt .45, and the open holster was tied to his thigh with a leather thong.

Johnny had heard him called gunslinger respectfully in the bunkhouse. He had heard him called killer and rattlesnake with no respect. Perhaps if it had not been for the mysterious and sinister tie between his father and Pfarr, Johnny might have admired the man, for natural is youth's inclination to admire violence and the men who live by it.

So is youth's consciousness strong of the strains and stresses that torment the minds of adults. Johnny was made uneasy by the strain in Ross. He hated the cynical and mocking surety in Pfarr. Sipping his coffee, Pfarr looked over the rim of his cup at Ross.

"I got your cut from the last bunch in my saddlebags," he said. "Remind me to give it to you."

Johnny could not miss Ross's look of pure, undistilled hatred, nor the venom in Ross McNaul's reply: "Pfarr, you can crowd a man too far. You can crowd a man until he forgets everything but the crowding. Remember that."

Leaving his breakfast untouched, Ross McNaul got to his feet, his mouth a slash in an angry and bitter face. He stamped out into the storm, leaving behind the undercurrents of uneasiness, a frightened boy, and a small, cruelly smiling man.

II

Saturday had passed. Sunday arrived, and the passage of the hours was measurable only in the way the snow increased its depth. All through the day the air was filled with the tiny, terrible flakes, settling inexorably downward. At 6:00 on Sunday night, snow on the level was at thirty inches, at 6:00 Monday morning at forty-two. And still it snowed. Sometime during the night, the wind had started again, whirling thick, blinding clouds of driven snow before it, scouring the high places, depositing this burden in the low places.

This morning, Ross McNaul took over a large part of Johnny's chores, wading through snow that reached nearly to his chest with Johnny stumbling along in his wake. The bunkhouse door, still sealed by snow, showed no indication of life from that quarter. Ernest Pfarr lay in the house, still rolled in his blankets.

After a full hour of fighting this weather, Ross McNaul and his son came back into the house, sweating and weary, to find Pfarr at the table sipping coffee.

Pfarr looked up. "Send the kid down to the bunkhouse, Ross. You and me have some talking to do."

Ross said, laying a hand on Johnny's shoulder:

"Go get Sikes and Joe up. Stay down there a while."

Johnny went out, scowling with a boy's resentment. When the door had closed behind him, Pfarr showed Ross his eyes, which had in them a sort of triumphant exultation. Pfarr said: "Ross, this storm is made to order. There is feed aplenty on the desert and the cattle could make it if they were started now. But if we let them go without feed for a week, it won't be possible."

Ross's amazement was plain in his glance. "Why you damned fool, you've made a good thing off these cattle. Why let them die?"

"We've been playing penny-ante so far. It's time to play for the big pot."

"And what is that?" Ross McNaul felt as a drowning man must feel, with the waters enveloping him, growing deeper over his head as he sank. Whatever plan the devious mind of Pfarr had now struck upon, it could mean nothing good for Ross McNaul.

"The ranch." Pfarr chuckled. "It came to me as I was lying in bed this morning. Old man Connors is dead. Judith Connors knows nothing about this ranch, nor how to run it. Her coming here, though, means that she's willing to try. We could change her mind for her, Ross. We could change it easy. Let the cattle mill around in the snow. Let her see them turn thin. Let her see them begin to die. Let her get up in the morning with the stench of dead flesh in her nose and let her go to bed with it at night."

Suddenly Ross shook his head. "No."

Pfarr smiled, saying with deceptive gentleness: "Why, all right, Ross. I can't make you do it. But call Johnny in. I've something to tell him about his pa."

Ross considered this, considered the falsely regretful face of Circle Dot's foreman before him, and suddenly more than anything in the world he wanted to shout: *Tell him, damn you! Tell him! He knows I'm afraid and he knows I'm ashamed. He's beginning to wonder why. He's too young to know what you and I have been doing, but he won't be too young long. Call him! It's better to lose him now, quickly, than to lose him a little at a time over the next ten years!* More than anything else, Ross McNaul wanted to smash his big fist into Pfarr's evil and smirking features.

Pfarr got up and moved toward the door. He opened it and stuck his head outside. He yelled: "Johnny!"

The wind blew its cloud of whirling white halfway across the room. In an instant all the warmth was gone from the room, and it was filled with the storm's bitter, insistent chill.

In his mind, Ross McNaul could see the horror that would come into Johnny's eyes, could hear his sobs and his piteous words: *I got to git out of here. I got to git away from him.* Ross jerked to his feet like a sleepwalker and strode to the door. He yanked it away from Pfarr and slammed it hard. He said: "All right. All right."

Pfarr took his heavy coat from the foot of the bed, shrugging into it wordlessly. He crammed his hat nearly to his ears. When he turned, his narrow-set eyes were hard and cold, his face unsmiling and grim. He said: "Ross, you're yellow clear through. I hate to trust you with this."

A flush rose into McNaul's features and his eyes glittered, warning Pfarr that he could go too far, yet in the little man was all the plain sadistic pleasure at setting the spurs deep into this man who could not fight back.

Pfarr went on: "I'm hanged if I'll spend the winter here. I'm going back to the desert while I can still get there. But don't get ideas, Ross. Don't think you can put anything over on Ernest Pfarr. Don't ever let a bunch of dead beef bring you to the point where you'll tell the boy yourself, because there's still something I can do to you. I can kill you, Ross. I won't bother to give you an even break. I'll shoot you down from behind."

Ross McNaul's eyes showed him nothing but pure hate.

Pfarr laughed. "There's another thing I can do, too. I can raise the boy for you, Ross, after I've killed you. I can raise him the way I'd like to raise him."

With fists hard-clenched, with madness in his

eyes, Ross McNaul advanced toward Pfarr, but the foreman ducked outside, colliding with Johnny on the stoop.

Johnny asked: "You call me, Mister Pfarr?"

Pfarr said—"No."—and laughed.

Ross McNaul stood futilely, helplessly in the doorway. Ross McNaul had seen a coyote once, held fast by a forefoot in a trap, could now remember how desperately the animal had gnawed at the imprisoned foot, trying to sever it. Admittedly this was the only solution for Ross McNaul. Johnny was a part of him, yet Ross's only hope of salvation lay in severing Johnny completely from him. He wondered briefly how long that particular coyote had waited, how long he had hesitated before he began his gnawing operation of severance. "As long as I have waited, perhaps," he said aloud.

Johnny turned from watching Pfarr as the foreman saddled his wet-backed horse. He asked: "What?"

"Nothing." Ross watched Pfarr ride out the lane, his stirrups dragging in the deep snow, his horse plunging against breast-deep drifts. At the open gate, Pfarr turned and raised a hand in mocking salute. Then he was lost in the whirling, drifting clouds of snow.

Johnny's voice penetrated his consciousness: "What you going to do about the cattle, Pa?"

"Why nothing, Johnny. Nothing at all. They will

make it or they won't." Pfarr was counting on a week of hesitation. After the week was past it would no longer matter. The cattle would die, either on the trail to the desert or here at the ranch. In a week, Pfarr's evil scheme would be a reality. The woman, Judith Connors, sickened by the stench of death, would seize upon Pfarr's niggardly offer for Circle Dot. Perhaps then Pfarr would be done with Ross McNaul and with Ross McNaul's son.

But Ross could not really believe even that. Men like Pfarr would always have a use for a strong and willing tool that was so utterly helpless in their hands. But the day must come at last when the stomach of Ross McNaul would retch and rebel at the chores Pfarr found for him. That day, at last, Johnny would know the truth and then there would be nothing left for Ross. Nothing at least but the killing of Ernest Pfarr.

Ross could look back, could see that his fatal mistake had been in taking Johnny at all. Johnny had been but a baby then, less than a year old. He would have thrived and grown without Ross. Ross could see that now. Yet at the time it had seemed the only thing, the only way he had of settling with his conscience.

You could raise a child, yet even if that child were not your own, he inevitably became a part of you. He became the source of your strength and the source of your weakness as well. He became a thing that to keep, you would lie for, steal for, cheat for, even kill for. And this was wrong, for out of such a relationship should come only good.

Stirred and tormented and turned unutterably sad, Ross McNaul caught the boy's thin body suddenly close to him, saying with unaccustomed hoarseness: "If anything should happen, Johnny, will you try to remember the good that has been between us? Will you try to do that?"

"Sure. Sure." The boy's embarrassment at his display of emotion brought a smile to Ross McNaul's long mouth. Eagerly, showing plainly his desire to ease the strain, Johnny piped: "Ain't this snow ever going to stop? Ain't it ever going to quit?"

But Ross did not answer, for his mind had again taken up its interminable wrestling with the problem that had no solution.

III

On Wednesday, with the snow depth standing at forty-nine inches in Wild Horse, the storm petered out and quit, but the skies remained overcast, gray and bleak, with low-flying clouds scudding past at terrifying speeds.

On Wednesday morning, Judith Connors donned boots, a man's Levi overalls and Mackinaw, and left her room in the hotel. The counterman in the hotel dining room came over to her table as she was eating breakfast, saying with some concern: "You ain't goin' to try makin' it out to Circle Dot, are you, Miss Connors?"

"I have waited three days. I could wait thirty more and there would still be snow."

"Snow'll be deeper at Circle Dot. Always is. Ross McNaul'll be in for supplies sometime this week. Wait for him."

Judith shook her head. She was a tall girl, tall enough to reach big Ross McNaul's chin. Her shining hair was not quite black. She could not tell this man the worry that was foremost in her thoughts. She could not say: *Father died leaving me nothing but this ranch and a lot of debts. I have got to see it. I have got to know what kind of a ranch it is.* Yet the concern and friendliness of this stranger put a warmth into her dark eyes, put a curve of pleasure into her lips.

He colored, saying as he untied the strings of his white apron: "You wait here, Miss Judith. I'll go down to the livery barn an' hire a sleigh for you. It ain't fitten fer a woman to have to wade them drifts."

"You needn't . . . ," she began, but halted in mid speech. She gave him her nicest smile then, and murmured—"Thank you."—for she had seen his disappointment at her protest.

With her breakfast finished, she went out into the biting air, standing on the hotel verandah to look up and down the street along the deep cañons that had been shoveled along Wild Horse's walks. A saddle horse plunged through the snow in midstreet, sweated and frothy, his rider retaining his seat with difficulty, for the plunging motion of a horse fighting through deep snow is different from any normal gait, and in this country the riders had no experience with it.

This rider had a red bandanna tied over his head and under his chin. Atop the bandanna his broad-brimmed hat sat, ill-fitting because of the added bulk of the bandanna.

The school on Wild Horse's outskirts stood cold and deserted, the snow surrounding it unmarred by any tracks or signs of life. An occasional pedestrian sidled down the walk, and mostly only their heads and shoulders were visible above the piled-high snowbanks. From the houses, from the stores along this street, rose plumes of smoke that hung low above the town before they drifted away on the wind to southward.

Bells *tinkled* downstreet toward the river, but it was a long time before Judith saw the sleigh, bounding and rocking and jerking along behind the team of plunging blacks. It drew up before the hotel and the counterman got down, covered with snow to his armpits before he could reach the verandah. The driver removed his hat and scratched his head. "I don't know. I don't know. It's twelve full miles to Circle Dot. I doubt if the team'll last that long."

Disappointment vied with Judith's sense of rightness, but she murmured staunchly: "I will not ask you to do it if you do not think you should."

The driver seemed to see her for the first time. *"Ahh,"* he said, "they can do it. Help her in, Ranse."

The horses fought and fidgeted, turned nervous by the unaccustomed depth of the snow, by the chill and wetness of it against their hides. Judith allowed herself to be lifted and carried to the sleigh, then settled herself comfortably beneath the mountainous pile of rough blankets.

The journey began, but it was late afternoon before they brought the low log buildings of Circle Dot into view, half buried in drifts. Long before they saw the buildings, they saw the cattle, bunched and miserable and hungry. At one place, close to the road, a cow nuzzled the still, cold form of her calf, and bawled plaintively. At another, Judith saw a cow, on her back in a drift, legs pointed straight at the sky, the snow about her giving mute evidence of her vain and useless struggles.

The buildings at Circle Dot, so bleak and plain, the never-ending valley with a thick and choking blanket of snow, the towering, grim, and threatening rims, all these things combined with Judith's nervousness and exhaustion, brought a suggestion of moisture to her frightened eyes.

She could not see the value of Circle Dot today. Today she could neither see nor visualize the thousands of acres of lush, waist-high grass that in summer was Circle Dot's golden treasure. Her thoughts cried out: *It's worthless! It's a wild, barren hole that is fit only for wolves.* She began to cry, her face buried in blankets to hide the tortured racking sobs that shook her.

But drawing up before Ross McNaul's small cabin, she presented to Ross and to his small, scared-faced son a dry-eyed, white-faced calm, and a small, timid smile. "I'm Judith Connors, and I guess you're Mister McNaul."

She could say the things that people had to say, but all she could think was: *Oh, how is this place going to pay Dad's debts? How can it give me a living? There is nothing here. Nothing. Nothing!*

Ross went wading out and lifted her down from the sleigh, then carried her into the cabin. At the doorway, he lifted his bellow toward the bunkhouse: "Sikes! Joe! Come, put this team up and give them a feed of hay." To the driver he said: "Get down and come in. Tomorrow is time enough for going back."

He stood looking down into Judith's face with almost abstract concentration. She was neither skinny, nor plain, he discovered, but she was tired and scared. She was warm and soft in his arms, and she stirred in this womanless man all of the hungers he had thought long ago forgotten.

She murmured: "Are you going to put me down?"

"Sure. Sure." Almost roughly he set her on her feet, flushing painfully. Turning his back, he went to the stove and brought the granite coffee pot forward from the back of it. His thoughts said: *Two more days and the week will be gone. She will make no suggestions before then. It will not occur to her that there is feed on the desert.*

Judith remained standing in the center of the room. Johnny stood with his back to the door, staring at her shyly. She gave him her smile, and he said: "Pfarr said you'd be skinny as an old gummer cow. You ain't."

Ross shouted: "John!" His face turned overly warm. Sweat glistened suddenly on his broad forehead. He poured a cup of coffee and brought it to Judith, whose smile was now fully amused, as she watched him openly.

Yet although Ross's embarrassment broke the sudden uneasiness, the catastrophic awareness that Johnny had not been present when Pfarr had spoken those particular words bothered his father. If Johnny had overheard that, then how much else had he overheard? This thought seemed to have occurred to Johnny, too, for his face turned dark red, and his eyes would not meet Ross's glance.

Nor did Judith Connors miss the interchange of suspicion and guilt that traveled between these two. Plainly misinterpreting the cause of it, she said to Ross: "Don't blame the boy. Children have a way of being more honest with adults than the adults are with them."

With startling suddenness, Ross McNaul fixed her with his stare, and the tortured thought ran through him: *What did she mean by that?* His common sense told him: *It was just a remark and it meant nothing.* Yet his uneasiness remained.

The sleigh driver, having seen to the stabling of his horses, now stamped into the room, shaking like a terrier emerging from water. "This storm will cost the country all that has been built up since the savages moved out. The cattle have started on the willow branches down by the creek. The danged stuff won't digest. Those that hunger don't kill will die from the wood pack in their stomachs."

Judith said: "The poor things. Is there nothing

that can be done? Is there no way to save them?"

Ross shook his head, drawing the scowl of the sleigh driver, who said: "There is feed on the desert. Cross Bar at Wild Horse began their drive yesterday. The others will follow."

Judith asked: "Can't we do that? Can't we do what the others are doing?"

Ross was nearly shouting as he replied: "No! Pfarr said no! It's crazy. They're too weak to plow through seventy miles of deep snow! They're too blamed weak, and I won't do it. You hear that? I won't do it!"

The liveryman, Slate O'Neal, murmured with some surprise: "Why, man, don't get excited about it. It is none of my affair and a thing to be thrashed out between yourself and Miss Connors and Pfarr."

Two more days. Two more days of waiting, and then, if Judith Connors's pressure became too great, he could start the drive. Ross said: "I'll build a fire in the house for you. Come along. Johnny. There will be sweeping to do."

He shrugged into his coat and banged outside with never a backward glance. But he could hear Johnny hurrying behind him, jumping and fighting and panting along in the deep snow. Johnny's voice was hoarse, quick with his short-ness of breath: "Pa, you figger the snow will melt on the south slopes? You figger the cattle will get feed without goin' clear to the desert, don't you?"

Ross did not answer, for he would not lie to the boy. He well knew that it might be a full month before the snow had settled and melted enough even on the south slopes to show these hungry cattle the grass and the ground beneath. He said: "Pfarr is foreman. He said to wait." He felt that even this was a lie.

"But Miss Connors is the owner, ain't she? Pfarr's got to do what she says, don't he?"

"Well, I reckon he does. But he isn't here now. He's down on the desert."

He reached the house and opened the door. It was cold and dark and dusty. He wiped a match alight on the sleeve of his heavy coat and raised the lamp chimney, touching fire to the wick. As the yellow light grew in the room, he crossed to the potbellied cast-iron stove in the center, began shaving a stick of wood with his knife.

He did not hear the brisk scratch of the broom on the rough floor and the roar of flame in the stove became only a background for his thoughts. He was back suddenly in that wild town on the Llano, wearing the silver star and carrying his authority slung low in its holster at his side.

IV

All men were wild on the Llano. They carried their law or their lawlessness in the guns at their sides. They settled their own disputes in burning powder and singing lead. Yet the new influx of immigrants from the East brought a different sort of men to the frontier, a soft breed that could not stand against the hard men of the high Texas plain.

Lacking the force of their own strength, these men brought a new force with them, book law, and hired the wildest of the wild to enforce it for them.

Ross McNaul was one of these, a big, quiet-faced man who rode the streets of Maverick, and with his own violence forced violence from the town.

The story was long. It dealt with a man's resentment against the inheriting of the country by these new and soft creatures from the East, these men who hired their fighting done, and whose purposes were often lawless and always greedy.

Johnny's father held a ranch on the Llano, held it the way all ranches were held in the early days, by squatter's right, and with no legal title. John Setter had been a friend of Ross McNaul's. Before his marriage he had ridden many a trail with Ross. He had settled down and taken up his ranch on the Llano at about the time Ross took the marshal's job in Maverick.

John Setter stood in the way. He held a water hole in the middle of what was to be a great ranch. So they moved him off—legally and very effectively. Resentment burned in John Setter, smoldered, and grew. Retaliation took the form of robbing the company bank in Maverick. Two men were killed.

Suddenly Ross McNaul's head began to ache, a violent pain that came whenever he thought of John Setter, of John Setter's wife and boy.

Ross McNaul's job had been to take John Setter. In his own steadfast way, Ross McNaul had believed in law, and this belief was the thing that had led him to accept the job as marshal in the first place. Much as he had hated this particular task, he had realized that law must be enforced against friend and foe alike or it becomes a useless and empty thing.

He had gone to the adobe hut where John Setter and his wife and baby were. He had found what he had not expected to find, that Setter's resentment had corroded him until he included Ross among those he hated because Ross enforced their law.

The rest was sordid and terrible. The inevitable shoot-out. The unexpected element, Setter's wife throwing herself in front of her husband just as Ross fired. A woman dead, a man dead, and a child that had become an orphan in seconds.

Squatted before the now roaring stove, Ross McNaul realized suddenly that Johnny was staring at him, with fright and puzzlement in his eyes. Ross passed a hand across his aching forehead, and at last heard Johnny's words: "Pa! What's the matter with you? Why don't you answer me?"

He got up with stiffness in his bones, with an odd light-headedness. He said: "Nothing's the matter, boy. I was thinking."

The thinking was not finished. That day he had quit the job in Maverick and to ease his conscience had taken the boy, then less than two years old. Later, much later, had come Pfarr, with his knowledge and his oily threats. Later, love for Johnny Setter had filled Ross McNaul's life, so that Johnny had become the only thing that mattered to him. Now he was trapped, and there was no way out. It was give up the boy, or give up forever the shreds of decency and self-respect that were left to him. What boy lived who could face the sudden knowledge that the man he had thought his father was not at all, was in fact the murderer of his real father and mother?

As it always did when he thought of these things, his head throbbed mercilessly, turning him dizzy, turning him nearly blind.

Behind him he heard the door open. He swung his head, saw Judith Connors shrugging out of her heavy coat.

Her glance at him was shy. She murmured: "I think it was very rude of me to question your decision regarding the cattle. I am sorry. You have much more experience in these matters than I, and I am sure you will do what is best." Because he did not smile, because his own thoughts had turned his face so grim and harsh, her smile faded.

Johnny said reprovingly: "Pa, you could tell her it's all right."

Suddenly Ross McNaul seemed to see Judith for the first time. She stood before him, her glance cool and straight, a woman lacking entirely in sham and coquetry, a woman soft and desirable, whose understanding might be even deep enough for Ross's problem.

So long and so speculatively did his glance dwell upon her that she turned uneasy. Johnny's words—"Pa, it ain't like you to act this way!"—beat dimly against his consciousness. Judith murmured: "You're a strange man. I think you must have something terrible living in your thoughts."

Almost dazedly he answered—"I have."—and went past her and out into the night. In the path he stumbled against a cow, and she lashed out at him with her heels, then floundering out of the poor path and into the deep snow.

Ross thought: *I can't do it. I can't stand by and watch Judith ruined.* But he knew he must.

• • •

At dawn, in bitter, sub-zero half light, Slate O'Neal began his return trip to Wild Horse with the sleigh. There had been no thawing of the snow, and so there was no crust. The path the horses and sleigh had made the previous evening was filled this morning with cattle, cattle reluctant to move again into the deep snow. Their heads hung dispiritedly, and their ribs had become a basket-work above which their hip bones protruded sharply.

Ross McNaul was ashamed at the relief that ran through him upon seeing their condition. "It is already too late," he told himself aloud. "They would never make the trip now."

Yet Pfarr had said a week. If Ross started the drive now, if some miracle happened and he got through with a portion of the cattle, then Pfarr's threat would become a reality.

Judith Connors came plowing down the path from the big house, flushed from the cold and very pretty. "There is not much that a woman can do here, but I want to do what I can. You and that boy have been cooking for yourselves long enough." Her voice was breathless from exertion, and her eyes took no recognition of his strange and set expression, of the haggardness upon his face.

This morning she wore a dress, fresh and bright as were her eyes, although rumpled from its long journey west in her valise. Her only concessions to the snow were the heavy boots she wore, and the thick and shapeless coat.

Johnny watched her with longing and hungry eyes, eyes that devoured and adored. Ross noticed that whenever Judith passed the boy, traveling between stove and table, she would touch him, gently, and at these times the boy would flush with pleasure.

Twice, she lifted her eyes to find Ross watching her. Perhaps she could see in him the hunger that the harsh years can put into a man, perhaps she saw the longing that was there, not because she was a woman, but because she was the particular woman. Perhaps it was the beginning of love that she saw in Ross McNaul's bleak features. Whatever it was confused her, but along with confusion was excitement, excitement that put a curve of pleasure into her lips.

She fed Johnny and Ross first, and, when Johnny was finished and had gone out to do his chores, she sat down at the table for her own breakfast, while Ross lingered over coffee beside her.

He watched her speculatively for a while over the rim of his cup, but slowly, inevitably his thoughts left her, his eyes became blank as his mind returned to the old ever-present problem.

Judith finished and stood up, began to clear the dishes from the table.

For pure courtesy's sake, Ross made conversation. "Would you have come out here if you had known it would be this bad?"

"Of course. Storms and snow are not exactly new to me, although I have never seen snow this deep."

"Most women would be reluctant to leave the East, would hate the hardship in the West."

"I had no choice. My father owned this ranch, but it was all he owned. He left me no money, only a lot of debts that will have to be paid. The ranch will have to pay them, and will have to feed me in the meantime."

Ross thought of the small-scale and quiet rustling that had gone on for three years now, of the share that he had received still cached untouched in a buckskin bag beneath his mattress. Guilt flooded him.

Starting with the shooting in the adobe shack in Maverick, everything he had touched he had soiled and cheated. Johnny first—now this girl.

In searching for a place to put the dishes, Judith suddenly and inadvertently opened the cupboard where Johnny's toys were stored. They tumbled onto the floor and she stooped to pick them up. Holding one, a tiny bear that Ross had whittled out one long winter's evening, she looked up, and there was the glistening of moisture in her eyes.

"Why they are things you have made yourself."

"Uhn-huh. Supplies are freighted to Wild Horse from the railhead at Antelope. It is mighty seldom that toys are included in the loads." Ross was frankly embarrassed and sought to justify the time he had expended in making these things. "The boy hasn't got a mother. He hasn't any other kids to play with. He's got to have something, I guess."

"Of course he does." There was an odd catch in Judith's voice. "It is the boy's mother that bothers you so, isn't it?"

"That's part of it, but only part."

She came over and lightly touched his arm. "Would talking about it help?"

For so long had Ross McNaul lived alone with this thing, for so long had he kept it bottled within himself, that the compulsion to unburden himself was nearly irresistible. No one could help, but perhaps Judith Connors could understand.

Ross was suddenly understanding himself that there was an end to it somewhere, an end that was inevitable and could not be changed. Johnny must know at last what Ross had done, and Johnny would hate him for it. Delaying Johnny's hate he could do, but only at the cost of his own self-respect, now nearly gone, only at the cost of ruining Judith Connors.

Suddenly he could no longer face the prospect of Judith Connors's ruin. Yet one more thing must be settled before he could talk. He said: "I have no right to ask anything of you. I have stolen from you and I have cheated you, but I have got to ask it anyway. Will you see to it that Pfarr does not get Johnny, after I'm gone?" He had been prepared for shock, revulsion, even hatred. All she showed him was amazement. His words tumbled from him. "He's a good kid . . . never caused me any trouble at all. I know it's a lot to ask, but I'm desperate. I can make it worth your while. I can help you out of this mess."

Judith said quietly: "Stop it. Johnny can have a home with me as long as he needs it. Does that help you any?"

Ross nodded his head in a puzzled way, but then he began to talk.

V

"I'm not his father at all. Eight years ago, I was marshal in a little town in Texas. Johnny's father got moved off his ranch, and because he resented it, because he was helpless, he made the mistake of robbing the land company's bank in Maverick. He killed two men doing it, and I got the job of taking him.

"I couldn't help it. It was one of those things that happen. He went for his gun and I went for mine. Johnny's mother must have thought she could stop it. She jumped between us and I killed her. The bullet went on through her and killed Johnny's dad."

Horror had widened Judith's eyes, but there was compassion in them as well, compassion for the torture so plain in Ross McNaul.

He went on: "There wasn't much in the way of families around Maverick then. It was a bad town. So I took the boy. I figured it was the least I could do. I didn't figure how much that boy would come to mean to me."

Now Ross's face turned hard and bitter. "I was punching cows for Cross Bar down at Wild Horse when Pfarr found me. He'd drifted away from Maverick, where he'd run a saloon when I was marshal. He knew what I'd done to Johnny's folks, and, when he saw how much I cared for

Johnny, he saw a chance to use me. He'd just been made foreman of Circle Dot and he threatened to tell Johnny about me if I didn't take a job here. That was the beginning. Since then, we have stolen about a third of your calf crop every year. Now he wants to steal your ranch."

"But how can he do that?"

"It is practically done. The cattle will die. He has figured that with the cattle gone, with no chance of income from the ranch, you will sell for little or nothing."

"But I won't!"

"*Ah,* you would have, though, if I had not told you what he meant to do."

Ross McNaul was not at all sure exactly what it was that her expression held for him. Yet he knew what she should be feeling.

Judith's voice was low, almost inaudible: "What can I do?"

"Nothing." Bitterness was full and hard in him. "Nothing at all. The cattle are finished. It is over seventy miles to Antelope, which is where the closest feed would be found. They cannot travel that far. There is not enough strength left in them."

"What will you do?"

"Ride."

"Where?"

"Over the pass to Antelope." He rose, and fished the heavy buckskin bag from beneath the mattress, tossing it on the table. "That is my share of the stolen cattle. I never wanted it. I did not steal from you for money. Perhaps it will help you some." He was thinking of Pfarr, he was thinking with some pleasure of the showdown, so long delayed, now so close at hand.

Judith must have read his expression for she said: "You're going to kill him."

He shrugged. "Or he will kill me. It is why I asked you to take the boy. Pfarr's latest threat was to kill me and take the boy to raise. You know what Pfarr would make of him."

Judith shuddered with distaste.

Ross heard a soft sound at the door, and swung his body violently. The door stood open perhaps an inch. In two strides he reached it and yanked it open.

Johnny stood there, and the thing in Johnny's eyes told Ross that the boy had heard. Johnny's eyes were flat, and cold, and hating.

Ross said—"Johnny. . . ."—and stopped. You do not reason with a child's hate, nor do you explain to it. For what seemed an eternity, Ross stared at the boy, and Johnny met his stare unflinchingly. Ross's voice then turned soft: "Will you remember what I asked you to do, Johnny? Will you try to remember the good things along with the bad?"

Johnny did not answer, nor did the set expression in his pale face alter. With the faintest of shrugs, Ross moved past him and went out the door.

Ten feet from the door he paused, tried to roll a cigarette, and failed. From the cabin he heard the boy's wild and sudden sobbing, heard the soft and sympathetic sounds that Judith made. He half turned to go back, but stopped himself, knowing at last the full, wild bitterness of loss. It was a thing a man could not fight. It was a thing he had to stand and take.

Almost running, Ross made for the corral, snatching his saddle and bridle from the barn as he passed through. Mounted, he took the rugged and drifted trail over the mesa. Ten miles this way— ten miles to Antelope and Pfarr.

For the first two miles the trail wound upward through cedar-covered benches. Ross's horse floundered and fought through the deep snow, sometimes slipping dangerously, sometimes nearly toppling over backward in his frantic effort to fight both snow and steep upward grade. A dozen times in the first mile, Ross dismounted, following behind the grunting and steaming horse.

Had he not known this old Indian trail so well, he would never have found it, could never have followed it at all, for truly amazing is the way four feet of snow can change the contours of a landscape, distorting or obliterating entirely most landmarks a man was accustomed to using.

In some measure he depended on his horse, that

also knew this way well. After three full hours of travel, he finally came out of the cedars and began the ascent of the narrow switchback trail that zigzagged across the steep bareness of the slide below the rim.

High brush, entirely buried by snow, made a dangerous trap for the horse if he varied so much as a yard from the marked trail. Once, the animal floundered into a thick pocket of this, and it took Ross a half hour of dogged and patient work to free him.

Inexorably and with infinite patience, he continued this inching and tedious progress, and at last climbed high enough on the slide to look downward into the cedar benches. At first he thought the dark, crawling spot there in the trees was a deer. Curiosity and the need for his horse to rest held him still, watching, and suddenly he knew that blob of darkness for what it was, a horse, bearing a pint-size rider. Johnny!

He cupped his hands to his mouth and shouted: "Go back you little fool!"

Almost he missed the high and piping shout that floated so eerily and faintly to his ears. Almost but not quite. The shout said: "If you can go over the pass, so can the cattle!"

Ah, the faith of a boy. Ross's horse, infinitely stronger than a steer or a cow, was near the end of his string. Ross yelled: "No! It can't be done! Go on back!"

He got no answer. Steadily the boy's horse forged ahead, reaching finally the flat clearing that stretched so emptily between cedar hills and the steep slide against the side of which Ross and his horse clung. Ross, growing angry at last, yelled again: "Go back! Hang it, do what I tell you!"

Ross knew the boy had heard, yet Johnny gave no indication. He never paused, or hesitated, just kept coming.

Ross swore bitterly beneath his breath, then resignedly reined around and took the downward back trail. Up to now he had not dared to hope that Johnny had forgiven, and, as he drew near to the boy, he could see the tight-drawn dislike that was there for him. Concern for Judith only then had prompted this boy's intervention.

Pride stirred in Ross. Riding up to catch Ross had been a difficult thing for Johnny; pleading with him would be harder. Ross tried to make it easier by saying: "It's no use, Johnny. They could never make it."

Johnny's horse fidgeted and pranced a little there in the trail, while Ross's mount stood head down, completely beat. Puzzlement flooded Ross's consciousness, puzzlement that could find no clarification because of his preoccupation with the boy. Johnny said, sullenly, his glance on his horse's withers: "If a trail was broke. . . ."

It made sense! It explained the freshness of

Johnny's horse in the face of the utter weariness that held Ross's still and head down. It was the thing that hung so puzzlingly behind Ross's thoughts.

When your mind has focused itself on one thing with a bitterness that surpasses all else, it is difficult to change. It was difficult for Ross to take his thoughts away from Pfarr, from the showdown, now but seven or eight miles removed. Yet as he considered these cattle, as he thought of the way Johnny's persistence had offered to them, excitement stirred him with its heady fumes.

Bringing the cattle into Antelope would be bitter gall to Pfarr. It would at the same time erase some of the evil of which Ross himself felt guilty. It would restore to Judith the chance to make of Circle Dot a living for herself, and for Johnny.

Ross McNaul said: "All right! Go on back down. Get Sikes and Joe out and start gathering the cattle. My horse is beat, and I'll be a good half hour behind you."

For just a short instant the hating stillness went out of Johnny's face.

Ross said: "Horses, too. Gather all the horses you can find. I'll help as soon as I can get there."

Excitement stirred Ross, just seeing the excitement in Johnny's face. The boy whirled his horse and plunged back downward through the cedars, using his heels to beat a rapid tattoo on the animal's ribs. Ross swung in his saddle and stared upward at the towering rimrock above. Blank, and harsh, and grim, it scowled back. It made its threat, it made its grisly promise to Ross.

Ross admitted this, that failure, disaster, and total loss of the cattle and of the lives of men were quite possible. Yet here was something a man could fight. Here was something to get his teeth into. Here lay a chance, however slim, to vindicate himself. What he had done to Johnny was buried in the past, and beyond changing. What he was doing to Judith might be changed.

He thought: *We'll drive a bunch of horses ahead to break trail. I'll beat Pfarr yet. By heaven, I'll beat him yet!*

Yet even his enthusiasm could recognize the chanciness of the undertaking. A slide could wipe them out, cattle and men. A misstep on the rimrock trail would be inevitably fatal for the one who made it. Exhaustion would render Ross himself more vulnerable in the final showdown with Pfarr at Antelope.

But Ross McNaul was not a man to harbor doubts any more and would not allow them to color or change his course. He turned his horse backward, and headed for the distant, tiny cluster of buildings that was Circle Dot.

VI

At nearly 2:00 in the afternoon, Ross came into the yard at Circle Dot, and he wasted no time, but off-saddled and immediately caught himself a fresh horse from the bunch in the corral.

Over a hundred cattle already milled inside the big corral, keeping their distances from the horses, staring with bovine placidity at Ross. They would look at certain death in the same placid way in which they now stared at Ross. They had neither the intelligence nor the will to try to change the workings of fate. A man was different.

Down the valley Ross could hear Sikes's harsh voice, Johnny's shrill one. He heard another voice, too, unmistakably a woman's, adding her cries to the clamor. The cattle were hungry and weak. They would be sluggish. Driving them over the pass would take much yelling and chap-slapping, would require whips and dogged persistence and patience.

Sinking spurs into his horse, Ross put the animal into a beaten path, and made his swift way toward the sounds of driven cattle. He saw Johnny, making a tiny and resolute figure atop his horse; he saw Judith Connors, shapeless in her heavy coat and Levi's. He reined his horse out of the trail, clinging like a burr as the animal

52

plunged through the virgin drifts, and then came up beside Judith.

Her face was flushed, her dark eyes bright, searching his face with an odd intensity. She asked: "Ross, can we do it, or are we foolish to try?"

He shrugged, for her question was but an echo of the question he had been asking himself.

Her glance lingered upon him, and became personal. Her eyes turned soft and warm, and she said: "Give the boy some time, Ross. Give him time to get used to the shock he has had. He will begin to remember how it has been between you. He will begin to understand that what you did was only what you were forced into."

Because her nearness could make the blood pound hard and fast in his veins his voice was gruff: "I doubt that." He added from some strange compulsion over which he had no control: "And you, what will you be thinking?"

He had the sense of Judith's withdrawal. She murmured: "I will be believing what I have tried to make Johnny believe. That men are drawn by circumstances into many things which are alien to their natures. You are not a man who could kill a woman except by accident. You are not a man who could steal unless the compulsion were overpowering."

Her eyes met and held his steadfastly. Under his searching glance they assumed a helplessness that was beseeching even while it showed her fear. It was woman's eternal invitation, co-mingling with woman's eternal elusiveness.

Johnny came up beside them, completely avoiding Ross's eyes, ignoring him with his words: "Sikes says this is all. Will we start tonight, or wait until morning?"

Judith deferred the question to Ross. "What do you think, Ross?"

"Morning. The pass is no place to be caught by night. I will take Sikes and go ahead at dawn with the horses. Joe can follow with Johnny and bring the cattle."

"Who will I ride with?"

He stared at her, his face stern. "You will stay here."

She gave him the faintest of shrugs. Sikes ran by, to open the corral gate. The cattle plodded into the yard, into the corral with little urging. Ross yelled: "Fork down hay that was to feed the milch cow! We will take her with us."

Judith dropped from her horse, and Johnny took her reins. She walked toward the cabin, and almost immediately after she entered it a smoke plume curled from its chimney.

Hay began to drop from the barn loft into the pole manger along one side of the corral, and, bawling and crowding, the cattle fought their way to it with frantic and starving greed.

It would not be much for four hundred cattle. It

would be but a full and warm feeling in them as they started the drive. But it might well mean the vital difference to many of them. Ross had not told Judith that they would be lucky to drive into Antelope half the number they started with. Yet he knew this was true.

Weariness put a sag to his shoulders, as he headed toward the cabin, with Johnny following sullenly behind. All this long day he had fought the snow, accomplishing nothing but the achievement of utter bone weariness. The exhilaration of the prospect of defeating the elements and Pfarr at once was gone before this exhaustion.

He entered the cabin, noting the pallor in Johnny's face as the boy entered behind him. This he had not considered, that the boy's day had been nearly as hard as his own. The words of comfort, the words of encouragement rose to his lips and died unuttered, and he said only: "Tomorrow will be a heller. A man'd be smart if he filled his belly and hit the hay. It is what I intend to do."

Johnny gave him a look that was only the brushing of his eyes against Ross and held no expression. The boy murmured: "Me, too."

Judith set the food before them, steaming, and Ross forced himself to eat, not wanting it, but knowing he needed it.

When the meal was over, Judith broke the silence with her words—"Good night."—and made her way up the path to the house. Johnny slipped out of his clothes and burrowed under his blankets without a word. Outside, the bunkhouse door slammed. A horse whinnied from the corral. A wolf howled, close by, and Johnny's dog began his shrill, terrified yapping. Already asleep, the boy stirred fitfully, and cried out. Ross went to him and laid a hand on his head.

A choked feeling came to his throat. He scowled and turned toward the door, going quietly outside into the bitter, clear, sub-zero night.

Wind whispered softly past the cabin's eaves, touched Ross's nostrils with its bite. He rolled a cigarette and held a match to its end. The smoke was a comfort in his lungs, a biting fragrance, familiar and good. Stars were a bright scattering of light in the velvet sky.

Snow *squeaked* under Judith's approaching feet. Her face was hidden from him, her thoughts secret because of this.

She seemed to feel the need of explaining her presence. "I couldn't sleep, Ross. I thought the air. . . ." Her words stopped, and for a long time she stared upward into the shadows that hid his face. Her nearness stirred the hungers that lay so close to the surface in Ross McNaul. Lightly she began to tremble, and Ross, feeling this trembling against him, knew that it was not caused by the cold.

It seemed to happen through no conscious movement on the part of either. It was one of those things that come about through mutual desire. She came against him, and his arms went out. As his hands touched her, felt her warmth and softness, all restraint went away from him. There was crushing strength in his arms. His lips became firm and hard and demanding.

What might have been the outpouring of sympathy in Judith he turned into desire that flamed as hotly as his own. She arched her back, her breath coming in short gasps. He sought to recapture her lips, but she eluded him, and buried her face against his shoulder, murmuring: "Ross. Ross." His name had a music on her lips. Yet it seemed to bring her a return of sanity. She said: "It would have been the same with *any* girl. You have been too long alone."

"No." His mind fought against her assertion that this was commonplace, that this could have happened to any but just the two of them. There had been other women in Ross McNaul's life, yet never had he experienced this overpowering sweetness. Urgent was his need to make her believe, and this urgency put power into his voice. "Judith, no. When I hold you close, my thoughts stop. I float a thousand miles above the earth. My blood runs hot. It's sweetness . . . and pain . . . and the whole world waits. Could it be like that with any girl?"

Her head tipped back. Her face was pale and still in the cold starlight. Because she said nothing, he pushed her roughly away. He said harshly: "You are thinking now of the things I have done. You are seeing me with a gun in my hand. You are seeing. . . ."

Before the bitterness in his tone she shrank away. Her protest had strength and the power to make him believe. "No, Ross, I stopped doubting you this morning. It is myself I doubt. It has got to be right, Ross. We have got to be sure."

His hands gripped her shoulders hard. His words had wisdom he did not know he possessed. "You have lost your father, and I have lost Johnny. It is human to seek to replace what we have lost. Yet there is more to it than that. I love you, Judith. I love you because your heart was big enough to understand and forgive. I love you because you were honest enough to come out here tonight because you knew I needed you." His arms drew her close; with his urgency he forced the blaze to kindle in her blood.

She melted against him; she became a part of him. When his lips found her face, they tasted the saltiness of her tears. His voice was tender and low: "Why, girl, it is not a thing to cry about."

Her laugh came, shaky and tremulous. "A woman cries when she is happy. Sometimes she laughs when she is sad."

Silence grew between them, with the calm and

peacefulness of their own thoughts, but gradually this silence changed, became charged with her fear and again she began to tremble.

She cried at last: "Ross, there are laws to take care of men like Pfarr. Let the law have him."

He shook his head. "I could let him go, but he would never let me go. You don't know him. He will avenge every real or fancied injury that is ever done him. He would wait for years, and suddenly some night a bullet would come at me from a clump of brush beside the road. Besides, there is nothing he has done for which the law would want him that I have not done, too. No, there can be but one end to this. If I do not kill him, he will eventually kill me."

Judith stiffened and withdrew. Her voice was cold. "There is a time when a man must stop living by his gun. I do not want a man who settles his troubles with bullets."

Strange and hard was the tension that settled between them. Ross had loved her because she could understand. He could not know that her present stand was wholly inspired by fear. She had sensed the deadliness, the killer instinct in Pfarr. She doubted that Ross could match it.

Coldly and wordlessly she turned, returning along the path to the house. Almost he called to her, but stopped himself. Eternal is woman's instinct to use the bargaining power of love. It is her only weapon. Eternal as well is man's resentment of woman's attempt to mold him into something less than he feels he should be.

Pride can be a force more powerful than love. Ross was discovering this. Yet, tonight, pride fled before Judith Connors's love. She came back along the path, repentant and shy. "I'm sorry, Ross. I was being a woman. It's only. . . ." She stopped, and then tried again. "I will not interfere. But be careful, Ross. Be careful. Please."

She was very near to tears. Before he could touch her, she was gone. For a long while he stared at the towering face of rimrock, black against the starlit sky, then with a light shrug, turned into the cabin.

VII

In ice-blue dawn, Ross swung to his saddle, feeling the chill of it against his legs, and sat beside the gate while Sikes hazed the horses, some twenty head, out of the corral. He lifted a gloved hand toward the cabin, where Judith and Johnny watched from the doorway.

A heavy woolen scarf was wound about Ross's head under his hat, coming down over his ears and tying beneath his chin. He wore scarred and heavy chaps; he wore canvas arctics over his boots. Beneath his heavy and shapeless coat, he wore his gun.

Once the horses were out, Ross had no time for thinking. It became a game, a game of out-guessing these animals that had no intention of taking any trail other than those which wound back and forth through the valley. Sikes stayed behind, crowding them, yelling. It became Ross's job to turn the leaders, to maneuver them into the trail upward toward the rim.

After half a dozen false starts he finally accomplished this, and, as they hit the steep upward grade, the running died out of them; they slowed to a plodding, steady scrambling.

Contrasting with the hours it had taken Ross yesterday to reach the slide, today it took them less than an hour. With his horse relatively fresh, here Ross took the lead, this being the only way in which he could eliminate the possibility of the horses taking the wrong turn, and, crowded from behind, plunging to their deaths.

He showed his saddle animal little mercy, spurring and pushing him all the while, and, when the horse tired, he off-saddled and caught a fresh one from behind him in the trail, then allowing his tired mount to join the bunch and proceed along a trail already broken.

A fresh horse lasted half a mile, but by this frequent changing, he climbed the miles away, and at 11:00 reached the bottom of the flat and foreboding face of rimrock, this sheer cliff that rose above him a full three hundred feet.

Here the trail was carved from solid rock, being never wider than two feet, being sometimes so narrow that a horse's ribs would scrape the rock as he trod lightly along the trail's outer edge. Ross would not permit himself to consider the things that could happen up there. He had seen horses lose their footing in dry weather and plunge hundreds of feet to the rocky slide below.

While he waited, giving the horses time to blow, time to restore the steadiness to their trembling legs, he stared down at the tiny and toy-like buildings of Circle Dot, at the slow, dark red stream of cattle that even now began the slow ascent through the cedars.

He could distinguish the tiny figure of Johnny,

the bulkier figure of Joe. He saw Judith Connors come from the house, and a few minutes later saw her appear, on horseback, in the trail behind the cattle. Soundlessly he cursed, and suddenly the cold chill of premonition traveled down his spine and raised the hackles on his neck. *I told her no! I told her she couldn't come!* He opened his mouth to shout, yet, knowing the uselessness of this, closed it, scowling.

Since a trail was already broken and it was unlikely that the cattle would deviate from it or exchange it for the trackless, deep snow, none of the three rode in the lead. But because there was danger that the leaders would stop, would balk in the trail, Joe rode perhaps a quarter of the distance back behind the leaders.

Her horse plunging and fighting along the edge of the broken trail, Judith took a spot a little more than halfway back, while Johnny brought up the rear. Ross nodded approvingly. Joe was a tough and seasoned cowhand. He had made a wise disposition of the forces at his command. The uneasy churning of fear persisted in Ross, but he forced his mind from Judith, from the things that could happen to her today, and raised his shout back down the trail at Sikes, the grizzled and unshaven Circle Dot hand: "Sikes! Wait up at the switchbacks, then if anything comes off, it won't take you with it."

This was an ever-present danger in winter on a

slick and winding trail. Ross had seen it happen. A horse would fall from the upper trail, and as he fell, bouncing on the trail below, would carry men and horses over the abyss each time he struck a switchback farther down. There would be no controlling the horses themselves. He had not men enough for that. But Sikes could protect himself. He could hold back until the way above was clear.

Ross started up, quirting and spurring his reluctant and terrified horse. His horse's fear was no ally here, for it only increased the chance that the animal would lose its footing. Ross kept his feet lightly in the stirrups, ready at each instant to leave the horse, to scramble to safety on the cliff side if the animal started to fall.

Rods became miles, and each mile was an eternity. The first switchback appeared below him, then the second. As he rounded the turn onto the third, he heard a scuffling fifty feet behind, and then the mortal, agonized scream of a horse.

He yanked himself around in time to see the horse, a big and shaggy bay gelding he knew as Shorty plunge into the abyss. Although he could not see this, he heard the solid and sickening crash as the horse struck the trail below, and suddenly, down there, heard another scrambling scuffle for footing, the shrill neighing of terror, and knew that at least one more had made the plunge.

At last, far below on the slide, he heard the *thump* as a body landed, another, a third, followed by the *rattle* of loose rock. He shouted: "Sikes! You all right?"

The reply was slow in coming, and when it came it was shaken and thin. "Yeah. Lord! *Phew,* that was close! Horse in front of me."

"How many?"

"Three countin' the one from up there. The rest are spooky. They're ready to bolt. By heaven, if they start to turn in the trail, you're goin' to hear some shootin'. They ain't a-goin' to crowd me off. Not me!"

"All right. Let's go."

Again the slow ascent began. On a jutting promontory, Ross looked below, seeing then the three shattered shapes of the horses, seeing the leaders of the stream of cattle warily entering the rimrock trail. He went on, and now he encountered the tracks of deer, the plain print of a wolf, and knew from this that he was very near to the top.

This was the worst side. From the head of this trail, a three-mile stretch of plateau lay before them, and then the trail descended again, descended through a rim like this one, but shallower and somewhat less sheer. Too, for some odd reason, perhaps because of the proximity of the desert, because of the warmer air, snow was never so deep on the other side. This, then, was the test. If they made it to the top with the cattle, it was likely that they would make the remainder of the journey in comparative safety.

He was thinking of Judith, trying to still the raw fear for her that ruled him so unmercifully. He was praying a little for her, too, in the incoherent way of a rough and untutored man.

Suddenly then, and with complete unexpectedness, he rounded a turn in the trail, and faced the upright and startled form of a black bear, a late hibernator, who had perhaps only a few minutes past left his cave for a look at the open countryside.

The bear presented no particular danger, for he was small, and as startled as was Ross McNaul. Yet the rank smell of him, the remembered and terrifying shape, turned Ross's horse suddenly and wildly frantic. The horse reared in the trail, snorting and wide-eyed. With a fist, slammed down hard between his ears, Ross brought him back to earth. He jerked tightly on the reins, by this trying to enforce his control of the terrified animal.

But as the horse had reared, so had he turned a little, and, when his forehoofs struck the earth, it was the side of the trail they struck, at a place where it sloped sharply into the void.

Backing and scrambling, the horse sought to reach firmer ground. The bear dropped to all fours and, turning, scrambled with ludicrous haste back up the trail into the close fringe of green-black spruce.

Ross's horse fought silently for his life. And in Ross, at a time like this, there was no thought of quitting the game creature. A shift of weight, the push it would take to clear him from the saddle, was also all that it would take to shove the horse over the edge. Ross raised a last shout—"Sikes! Get clear!"—and put every ounce of his own strength and balance into helping his mount.

On a dry trail he might have made it. In slippery and unpacked new snow there had never been any real chance. The horse's forehoofs went off, and for an endless instant he lay, belly and hind feet on the trail. The dropping of his forehoofs had thrown Ross forward in the saddle. Now, with an explosive motion, he put every bit of strength in his body into throwing himself back. His body reared upright in the saddle, and a leg flung over it. The horse slid from beneath him, screaming, turning end over end as he fell. Ross lit on his back across the trail, his heels driving at thin air, and inch by inch slid toward the edge. He tried to roll, to get himself on his stomach so that his clawing hands might get a purchase in the loose snow. He only hastened his sliding progress.

His horse struck the promontory below and caught there, his belly tearing open on the jagged rock. Sikes raised an agonized shout at the sight of Ross's saddle on the animal's back. "Ross! Oh, Lord, Ross, hang on!"

Ross heard none of this. There was an instant that he knew he was going over, an instant when he knew there was no stopping this. And as often happens, he could face it with calmness he would not have believed possible. With a shrug that was entirely mental that had no time in which to transfer itself into the physical, he felt the last touch of rock at his back.

Then he was falling. There was the empty nausea of this briefly in his stomach. From a terrifying distance he heard a scream, a lost and eerie wail that lifted from the trail two-thirds of the way down the rim's sheer face.

Thin, empty air surrounded him. He was floating. This was as death must be, this lack of physical sensation other than that of complete weightlessness. His mind was blank and he waited, waited for the crushing impact, for the brief pain that would come as his body broke on the rocks.

VIII

For Judith Connors, nothing east of the Mississippi could match the terrifying grandeur of this land, this mesa that rose from the valley floor, this face of rimrock, so sheer, so tall, so utterly and grimly magnificent.

Hemmed in completely by the cattle before her, by those behind, she let her horse's reins go slack, and lifted her eyes to watch the ant-like progress of Ross McNaul above, the single-file bunch of horses that followed him, Sikes, the grizzled Circle Dot cowpuncher, bringing up the rear.

Her throat was raw from her shouting, her thigh smarting from the repeated slap of her gloved hand. The cattle were not like the horses. Their progress was slower, their hesitations more prolonged.

From the clearing at the foot of the slide, Judith had seen the awful plunge that the three horses made, had heard their lost and frantic screams. Now, entering the rimrock trail, she could look fifty feet below her and see their bloody and broken bodies.

Terror laid its clammy hand over all her thoughts, terror for herself, for Ross, for the boy, still behind her so white-faced. This ride seemed a nightmare, that had no ending save that of the plunge through space, the impact of her body against rock.

Seemingly inch by inch the cattle climbed. Before her, the cowpuncher Joe, his coat pocket loaded with rocks, cursed and fumed, and pitched the jagged rocks at the leaders whenever they would halt their plodding progress. At a turn in the trail, Judith looked up, saw Ross McNaul, tall and still on a promontory of rock, watching her.

Courage seemed to flow to her from him. She smiled and lifted an arm to wave. He returned her wave, reined his horse on.

Judith saw the black dot up there that was the small bear before Ross did. She watched it curiously, not knowing what it was, never dreaming of the havoc it could cause.

She saw Ross's horse approach it, saw it halt, saw it rear. There was unreality, a stage-like quality to this, as though it were not really happening.

As Ross's horse reared, a scream froze in Judith's throat. She saw the animal come down in response to Ross's instant and brutal blow, and briefly relief touched her. The bear disappeared, but now Judith could see the fight that Ross's horse was making, his scrambling fight for footing.

Ice congealed about her heart as the horse's front hoofs went off the edge. Her breathing stopped as he hung there. The horse came off the trail, riderless and seemed to float briefly in space. She heard Sikes's yell, and waited, seeing the tiny spot that was Ross fighting so silently up there, legs flailing against thin air.

Then Ross, too, came loose from the trail, his body turning in air. It was then that the scream broke from Judith's bloodless lips. It lifted to Ross and went on, to bounce against the wall of rock and return to Judith, an echo, a lost and terrible echo.

Neither Ross nor the horse plunged all the way. The horse struck the promontory upon which Ross had stood but moments before, and the sound it made was heavy and audible to Judith, even away down here. She could not see where Ross struck. He simply disappeared.

Judith doubled in her saddle, burying her face in her arms, shuddering uncontrollably. There was light and faint sound behind her, a thin, choked cry, and then silence.

Remembering the boy, she swung in her saddle, separated from Johnny by the backs of a hundred cattle, unable to give him comfort. Johnny's face was drawn, nearly blue in color. His eyes were wide. His breath came in gasps that seemed to cause him pain.

Her lips gave voice to the cry of her heart: "Johnny! Johnny! Don't give up hope. Johnny, please!"

He stared at her with no seeming comprehension. His lips worked but issued no sound. The cattle plodded on, inexorably, at last taking what seemed to be the entire trail, making a serpentine column back and forth nearly to the top. A weak one toppled and fell, carrying half a dozen with her before she reached the bottom, yet even this now left Judith unmoved.

Above her the horses went on, and after what seemed an eternity Sikes reached the promontory where Ross McNaul lay, dismounted, and disappeared himself. Judith screamed: "Sikes! Sikes! What is it?"

His bellow came down, giving hope but no details: "He's alive!"

Judith hated the cattle suddenly, hated them for bringing this about, hated them for standing between her and Ross, blocking the trail as effectively as would a monstrous wall of rock. She hated herself for allowing Ross to undertake this hazardous journey, when all the while she knew in her heart that she could never have stopped him once his mind was made up. She prayed. She suffered with Johnny, knowing what agony worked in him, knowing that forgiveness was in him to give to Ross, and that it was almost certainly too late.

The horses disappeared unattended into the spruce fringe atop the mesa, and the head of the column of cattle followed. Like a thin, sinuous worm the stream of cattle entered the timber, were swallowed into its secret blackness.

Noon came, and the day waned. Sikes's bellow came at last: "He's conscious! Ribs maybe. Back maybe. I don't know. He bounced on the horse and lit in the snow."

Behind her Johnny released a sigh, and she knew the reason for this. There was hope in the boy now, hope that he might make his peace with the man before he died.

Judith said in a low and beseeching voice: "Lord, he's paid for all that he's ever done. Let him alone now. Let him alone."

She drew near to the promontory and the tension in her increased. She reached it at last, slid from her horse, almost falling, and stumbled to where Ross lay, a cigarette dangling from his slack lips. He made a wry grin at her through the pain that racked his breathing, saying: "We've got it made now. A damn' fool thing to do. A fool thing."

Judith cried silently, fearing to touch him, but wanting to. Sikes rose and broke up a knot of cattle that was building at this bend in the trail. The last of them went past, and Johnny came running and falling and crying to throw himself down beside Ross.

"You hurt? You all right? Oh, Lordy, Pa, I'm sorry. I did what you said, all the way up here. I remembered the good things, Pa."

Judith turned away. Sikes coughed. Joe came

back with a couple of poles, dragging them laboriously down the now well-packed trail. As Judith watched, he rigged a travois by lashing rope supports across the poles and, when it was done, lashed one end of the thing to the saddle of his horse.

Sikes went back to Ross, saying gruffly: "We got to bind them ribs. You think it's ribs, or your back?"

Ross sat up, the effort of it bringing a heavy film of sweat to his face. "Ribs," he gasped. "That's all."

He was thinking of Pfarr, and of Pfarr's threat: "I'll shoot you down from behind."

He knew the end to this, for there was no longer any chance that he could beat Pfarr to the draw. But he had seen men who could trigger a gun two or three times, dead on their feet. He could kill Pfarr if he wanted to badly enough. He could kill Pfarr while the man's bullets were tearing into him. It was either this, or wait for the bullet that came from the roadside. Life and the workings of fate seldom gave a man his living the way he wanted it. Yet there were a few forks in the road, and the way you were made invariably determined the turn you took. . . .

Across the mesa top, nearly prairie flat, wound this exhausted and drained procession. A breeze warm as a Chinook blew in from the desert, whose

74

flat and endless expanse lay before and far below them. It brought the horses' ears pricking forward; it put new energy into the cattle. It packed the snow, and it made the trail slippery.

Yet ever the downward way is the easy way. The forward-pointing cloven hoofs of the cattle pushed themselves into the packed snow and gave firm purchase. Neither was this trail as steep. Neither was the distance through the rim as long before the gentle sloping of cedar-covered benches began. Reaching these, Ross, on his jolting travois, knew that the worst was past for the animals, for Judith, for the boy.

On the desert floor, less than a foot of snow remained, and, as they traveled across this almost flat expanse, it grew ever less, until the bareness of the ground showed through in the high places. The cattle now became entirely unmanageable. They bunched on these bare spots, clearing them of grass swiftly, then moving on to the next.

Ross shouted: "Drop 'em! Let them fill their bellies. They'll be here tomorrow. They'll be here for a long while."

So they left the cattle. They left the horses, save for one that Ross made Sikes rope out of the bunch. He slid off his travois, and walked stiffly away. He said: "Sikes, ride that one bareback, and let me have your saddle. I'm hanged if I'll go into Antelope on my back."

Judith protested, but it did her no good. Johnny

was strangely silent, and Ross had the feeling that the boy knew what lay ahead.

The small, squat cluster of buildings comprising the desert town of Antelope appeared on the horizon, and grew slowly as they approached. So did the tension grow in Ross. They would want to put him in bed. They would want him to be examined by a doctor. If they knew what was in his mind, they would want to stop him.

Night came down, soft, warm by comparison to the high country above Wild Horse. Stars winked in the graying sky, growing brighter as all light faded from it.

The good of success made warmth in Ross. The feeling that he had been instrumental in saving Judith's cattle took away much of the bitterness of his pain, of his exhaustion.

One thing only was left for him to do success-fully. Yet Pfarr could be infinitely more deadly than the elements; Pfarr was a force that only death could defeat.

At the edge of town, Sikes rode up beside him, saying: "I've heard the story from the girl. Pfarr will be hard to face. I guess I'll come along."

Ross shook his head no and was silent, watching Sikes edge back ahead. Then he dropped behind, gradually, and, when the black of invisibility separated him from the others, cut away from the trail, taking then his own separate way into Antelope.

IX

Everything about the town of Antelope was flat. It was comprised almost exclusively of flat-roofed adobe buildings, drab and squat and without beauty. Antelope had no street pattern save for the one main street that ran its straight way through town. For the rest, alleys and lanes meandered about, serving in their roundabout ways each separate building or shack.

Customarily saloons clustered together at one end of the main street that bore the name Mesa Avenue, while at the other end were the substantial stores of the town, and farther the residences of their owners.

Antelope lived because it was the terminal of the railroad, a shipping center in the fall, a buying center for the vast country to eastward, the Wild Horse country and beyond.

Ross McNaul entered it at the lower end of Mesa, holding his horse at a leisurely walk. For days there had been a particular urgency about all Ross had done. Tonight that urgency was gone. This was a task that could not be hurried, for hurry begets mistakes, and Ross could afford none of them. *A close thing,* was his thought. *This will be a close thing however I figure it.*

There had been a day, in the haze of the past, when Ross McNaul could have faced Pfarr with no doubt of the outcome. In Maverick, challenges to Ross's gun speed had been infrequent.

Yet on the day he had killed John Setter and John Setter's wife, Ross McNaul had put aside his gun, had stopped abruptly the daily exacting practice in drawing and firing that is a gunman's life insurance. Not until the coming of Pfarr had he again worn it.

Conversely Pfarr had apparently built up his skill over the years. There had been a day, back on Circle Dot, when Ross had come upon him, unseen and unnoticed, and had watched Pfarr's performance of the gunman's daily ritual. The drawing, the firing, the speed with which five bullets could be dispatched, the number of them he could put into a tin can at twenty-five feet. Close-range man-killing practice.

In this early evening darkness, lamplight twinkled from the stores, cast a dim pattern on the ground before the grimy windows of the saloons. The street itself was a sea of mud. Snow lay along the north sides of the stores, and now, with the chill approach of night, the mud of the street turned firm and began to crust with frost. By morning the whole street would be frozen solid, each rut and track preserved, until the thawing of the following day, and the churn of new traffic obliterated them.

Ross dismounted, strongly feeling the weariness of the day in his bruised and broken body. He tied the horse, moved upstreet with careful steps, finally putting the point of his shoulder against a saloon wall to steady himself as he formed a cigarette. The door beside him banged briefly open, and a man came out, flushed with alcohol, walking with the peculiar deliberation and care of a man in his cups.

Ross asked—"Got a match, friend?"—and saw the man start, saw him swing. Ross said: "I'd like to find Pfarr, foreman of Circle Dot up at Wild Horse. You know where he'd be?"

The man fumbled fruitlessly in his pockets, cursing softly. He came up with a match at last and thumbed it alight, then holding it toward Ross and peering curiously.

Ross stuck his head forward, put the end of his smoke into the flare. "Well?"

"Ain't seen him tonight. He hangs out in the Silver Dollar, three doors down the street an' on this same side."

Ross muttered—"Thanks."—and watched the man stumble away. He saw the small cluster of Circle Dot horses tied a block away before the unsubstantial and sagging frame hotel, recognized them, and knew that interference from Johnny and Judith and the others was but minutes away. As he turned down the street, Johnny came onto the hotel porch and stared into the dimness downstreet without seeing Ross.

Knowing now where to look, with the need to

hunt through each saloon gone, Ross shoved himself away from the wall. For a short instant he stood very still, using this time to put the force of his will against the pain of his body, against the utter weariness of his brain. Then walking as though each vestige of hurt had been banished, he went the short distance down Mesa and pushed open the door of the Silver Dollar.

The familiar pattern of this became a sense of repetition in him. Many times in Ross's life had this same scene acted itself out, yet always before the silver star had adorned Ross's vest, had given him the authority of being right. He gave his head an imperceptible shake, and his head swiveled with its appearance of idle curiosity. Upon his brain the scene was etched indelibly. He saw the three who sat at a poker table against the wall, the dark-faced swamper who dozed against the same wall, broom propped up beside him. He saw the four at the bar, and studied the face of each as it was turned toward him. He saw the odd expression that traced across Pfarr's seamed features.

He centered his attention on Pfarr, yet at the edges of his vision remained these others. If they sought to become a part of this, he would know it.

He spoke deliberately, with the old chest tightness of impending action squeezing him: "I brought the cattle over the pass, Pfarr. They're safe, all but a dozen or so that didn't make it."

Pfarr pushed himself away from the bar, turning his body slowly and deliberately toward Ross.

Ross said: "Johnny knows about me, and so does Judith Connors. There is nothing left for you but the gun, Pfarr. Use it."

Pfarr seemed to crouch at his words. Ross's subconscious told him: *Now. Now. Give yourself a little edge.* Yet he could not move his hand. Knowing his skill, Ross had never in his life drawn his gun against another man first. The habit had become too deeply imbedded to change it now.

He waited and the split part of a second that remained dragged itself out until it became an endless thing, a space of time in which there was only intolerable tension. The enforced buildup of hate and frustration was very visible in Pfarr, and this was the difference between these two. Pfarr would always need the stimulation of desperation to speed his draw; Ross would ever remain cool.

The men at the bar sidled down it away from Pfarr. The game against the wall stopped and turned silent. The swamper stirred. The bartender moved away from Pfarr, saying nervously— "Outside. Take it outside boys."—plainly knowing that no one would heed him, not particularly caring.

Ross let his shoulder stir, for a point of pain stabbed itself upward from his shattered ribs. Pfarr had been watching his eyes, and suddenly his expression tautened. Briefly his eyes turned strange with fear. His hand dropped, his shoulder with it, and his crouch deepened. He had thought Ross's shoulder movement was the beginning of his draw, and his haste was frantic. His gun was half out of its holster, hammer back, before Ross could stir.

Then the old, automatic things so deeply ingrained in Ross took hold. With no conscious effort or movement, he felt the smooth grips of his gun under his palm, felt his thumb against the hammer.

Pfarr's shot blasted, its acrid cloud of black powder smoke mushrooming out before him. Ross's gun came up. Pfarr's second shot hit against Ross's shoulder like the blow of a fist and stopped the upward swing of Ross's gun. Pfarr's third bullet took Ross's right leg out from under him, and he felt himself falling.

Desperation rose, and the red curtain of rage. From the floor, Ross saw the dip of Pfarr's gun muzzle, saw the hammer thumb back for the fourth shot. He looked directly into the wide and black muzzle of Pfarr's gun, with a part of his mind knowing that Pfarr was aiming this for his head.

He rolled, and watched the deliberate way in which Pfarr's gun muzzle followed. He snapped his gun up, his position awkward, but knowing at last with a gunman's instinct that this shot would be right, would be right at least if he ever got it off. Pfarr's finger tightened on the trigger. Ross pulled his, a fine-action trigger with a purposely easy pull. His gun bucked, but he continued his roll. Sure as he had felt, he could afford no less than all the chances he had.

For an instant, Pfarr showed no change. Then he jerked convulsively. His gun wavered minutely and went off. The bullet tore into the floor a foot from Ross's head. Ross brought his feet under him, rising to his knees as Pfarr fell.

He could feel the wetness seeping down his arm from his shoulder. His leg was warm and wet. The old wildness came back as he crouched there, and he swung his gun muzzle, saying his savage invitation: "Anyone else? Anyone want to take it up?"

The bartender murmured: "Easy now. One is enough."

"All right." Weakness overwhelmed Ross. Numbness began to leave shoulder and thigh, and pain began. His sharp exertion had brought on excruciating pain in his ribs. The murmur of voices faded and became vague, then blanked out before the roaring in his ears. This was death, he decided, and could feel no bitterness, because he knew Pfarr had preceded him. . . .

The doctor straightened. Ross McNaul lay face down upon the hotel bed, stripped to the waist, a thick wad of bandages wound around his torso. "Wonder he didn't puncture a lung with those ribs. Lucky." He turned a sour scowl on Judith Connors, on young Johnny McNaul. "Dry your tears," he said. "He's too mean to kill."

He turned and closed his bag with a snap. Going down the creaking stairs he grunted: "Lucky more ways than one." He was remembering the beauty of relief in Judith Connors's face. He knew he could never forget the glory in young Johnny McNaul's. He muttered again: "Lucky man."

These were the compensations of the rough and thankless life a doctor led in a frontier town, the abject thanks of a woman when he saved her man, the adoration of a boy. A doctor stored these things, banked them against the future, drew against them often to cancel bitterness and despair. As he paused at the bottom of the stairs, Judith's glad weeping drifted softly down, and, as he went away, the doctor smiled.

★ ★ ★ ★ ★

Savage Desert

★ ★ ★ ★ ★

I

He found it in late afternoon, stagnant and green with moss. But it was water, enough for the thirsty, sweaty teams, enough for the men, enough by morning to fill the water casks. And he headed back at once.

He rode loosely, did Sam Duke, loosely with weariness that expressed itself in every line of his big, bony, hard-muscled body. Reddish whiskers stubbled his dusty face. His eyes were red from the glare of the desert sun. His tan, wide-brimmed hat had a dark streak of sweat around the base of its uncreased crown.

The lines of his face were harsh. Jutting, bony chin, hollow cheeks with high cheek bones as prominent as those of a Cheyenne chief. His eyes, chill blue, were sunken deeply in their sockets and rimmed with a thousand tiny wrinkles born of squinting against the glare. His forehead was high and smooth. The hair, growing long at the temples and over his protruding ears, was touched with gray.

Sweaty, faded blue shirt. Dark blue cavalry pants with darker streaks along the seams to show where the yellow stripes had been. Texas high-heeled boots with Spanish cartwheel spurs. And a gun sagging against his thigh on a cracked, worn cartridge belt.

The horse traveled at a steady, bone-jolting trot, but the man rode it smoothly and without discomfort. It was an easy gait for the horse, one that covered the miles without really wearing him down.

And the miles dropped steadily behind. There was a road through here of sorts. It followed the contours of the land, winding around obstacles, detouring high ground. A seldom traveled road, but a road nevertheless. Wiped out in spots by the scouring desert wind. Plain where it was sheltered from the wind.

The sun sank steadily toward the rocky line of jagged hills in the west, the hills they must cross tomorrow. Ahead of him it stained high-floating clouds with fire that quickly died to the gray, dead ashes of dusk. And in dusk, late dusk, he reached the spot he had left them mending a broken wheel.

Ashes of a fire to one side of the road. Lumped shapes like sleeping men upon the ground. But no wagons, no horses, no mules.

He spurred his horse, a sense of disaster touching him. He rode at a pounding gallop toward the scene.

Long before he reached it his eyes verified that which they had only guessed before. The fire was dead. The men were dead. And the wagons and teams were gone.

There was shock in the man at first, shock that grayed his face and bewildered his blue eyes. He went from one to another, searching, peering into their faces, sometimes turning one that lay face downward on the ground. He knew each one; he had covered five hundred miles with them. And then he came to the one for whom he sought.

This one was slight, with a shock of reddish hair similar to Sam's. Only untouched with gray. And the face unlined.

A shudder touched Sam's rugged, bony frame as he knelt there in the dust beside his brother's body. A shudder that seemed almost like a chill.

A callused hand came down and touched the pale, dead face. A flood of grief, of anger and outrage beat against the dam of restraint within the man. He blinked his eyes and swallowed. He cleared his raspy throat.

No questions yet. But they would come. Who? And how? When? And why? Those were questions his mind would ask. Those were questions he would have to have answers for.

Almost dazedly he stumbled to the fire and restarted it from shavings and from a pile of wood gathered previously. Then, in the light of the fire, he studied the site with eyes stunned by both shock and grief, but beginning to show the smoldering fire of a terrible anger.

Indians had not done this. The bodies were not mutilated. Indians might have stolen the horses and mules. They might have rifled the wagon goods searching for things they could use. But they would not have driven the wagons away. They would have burned them here.

White men then. White men so savage they could wipe out a dozen of their own kind solely for the things they possessed. It explained why there was no evidence of a fight. Sam's brother and his teamsters had let the killers walk unmolested into camp.

No shovel with which to dig. But one of the men had a large sheath knife with a long, wide blade.

He slid it from its sheath, left the body of its owner, and began to dig, loosening the ground with the knife, clawing it out with his hands. He dug steadily, silently.

A single grave for his brother Claude. A common grave for the others. Neither of them deep. Only deep enough for the bodies and for a shallow covering of earth.

The hours passed. Sweat soaked his clothes and the night was cool. Dawn came streaking the flat horizon to the east as he finished his grisly task.

His fingernails were gone. And his hands were a mass of blood. A wind was rising now, stirring clouds of dust from the high points of ground it swept across.

It would scour the ground. It would sweep away the tracks. But not all of them. Not every track. In sheltered spots they would remain, and where they remained he would find them. If it took him the rest of his life.

He had no Bible, but he stood for a moment over the fresh-stirred earth, hat held in his two hands in front of him. He said, drawing these words from vague memories of another time: " 'The Lord giveth and the Lord taketh away. Blessed be the name of the Lord.' " His voice was cracked and hoarse. He stared at the single grave. "I'll get 'em, Claude," he said. "I'll get every damn' one of them for you if it takes me the rest of my life."

He turned to his horse and mounted.

Circling now, he watched the ground carefully, and, when he found the deeply indented tracks of the seven wagons, he turned that way and followed.

This was to have been a new freight line—a new start in the freighting business at the end of the journey from the East. These were the things they had planned.

Claude would have been twenty on his next birthday. He'd stayed at home through five long years of war, working the farm, caring for their ailing parents. Lung fever took them both in the winter of 1864. When Sam reached home after being mustered out, Claude had buried them and was near to death himself.

The trek westward through the desert was to have restored his health. Instead it had taken his life. And Sam was all alone.

A man has ties, he thought, *that inevitably*

break. But as each one breaks, the others become stronger. And when the last one snaps. . . . His face set itself in grimmer lines.

What kind of men were these he followed now? What kind of men could walk into an unsuspecting camp and cold-bloodedly execute every man in it? He shook his head. Death he had often seen. Mass slaughter he had seen as well during the terrible long years of the war. But that had been done in the name of patriotism, for a cause. Men on both sides had at least believed they were right.

This was murder for gain, the work of butchers. But they had made their first mistake. Somehow they had missed his tracks going on or had simply assumed that no one escaped. They had thought they got them all.

Seven wagons were too big to hide. The wind would not completely destroy their tracks. On casual appraisal, finding them would seem to be a simple task.

And perhaps it was. Yet something told him he was not on the trail of fools. Somewhere, sometime the trail would disappear.

In spite of this certainty, no worry touched or softened the lines of his face. They had made their first mistake. They would make a second— and a third.

The sun came up, bright as shining gold, and bathed the land with its changing dawn colors, then started its climb across the sky. Heat waves rose from the land, shimmering, distorting the shapes ahead. The man rode doggedly on, his eyes mostly upon the ground but occasionally lifting to sweep the country that surrounded him. There would be no vengeance if he let himself be surprised by Indians, if he let himself be killed.

And he thought of the men he pursued. He savored the vengeance he had promised himself.

He would kill them one by one. He would kill them, but only after he had told them why.

The land changed as he rode. It was hotter, drier. There was less vegetation. And it was flatter, too. The rising wind had almost swept out the trail.

Tomorrow there would be nothing—no wagon tracks—nothing a man could follow long. The wagons, the freight, the thieves would be lost in the endless plain.

His horse was streaked with drying sweat. He labored to walk, and breathe. Heat beat down upon Sam and his mouth felt like dry cotton.

Vegetation petered out. He rode into a bleak expanse of dry lakebed and squinted against the glare of it.

A pile of rounded, blackish boulders offered shade and he turned toward them, dismounting as the sun reached its zenith in the sky. If a man squatted close against a face of rock, led his horse against another, both could rest briefly in the shade. Sam got his canteen from the saddle, poured some water into his hat, and let his horse suck noisily at it until it was gone. He took a brief drink himself, corked the canteen, and restored it to its place on a saddle. He squatted in the shade, his craggy face expressionless.

He had suspected he would lose the trail. Now he knew why he would. Wind must blow forever in this parched, hot land. And here, where there was no shelter, it would soon obliterate the trail.

Another enemy faced him. Thirst. There could be no water here. Only that which he carried in his own canteen.

He let his horse rest until the animal stopped heaving and began to breathe normally. Then he mounted again and rode out at a plodding walk.

The lakebed stretched ahead of him like a sea that had no end. He traveled mostly by direction, casting back and forth occasionally to search for trail. Sand sifted into it like drifting snow and it became, as the afternoon progressed, more and more difficult to find.

But as the sun sank in the western sky, as the air briefly cleared, he saw ahead of him the barely visible, circling dots in the sky that could be but one thing—vultures.

Directly ahead. He must decide right now whether to stop following trail and head for the birds, or whether to follow slavishly until the light faded and it became impossible to see.

Tomorrow, the trail would be gone. Wind, blowing throughout the night, would scour the land completely clean.

He hesitated only a moment. Then he urged the weary, dried-out horse to a jolting trot and headed directly toward the circling birds.

It was sundown when he reached the spot, which lay in a mile-wide hollow that had, apparently, once been the center of this lake and deeper than the rest. He stopped on its rim in disbelief.

Wagons. There must be well over a hundred of them. Whitened. Bleached. Sand-blasted by the wind and sometimes half buried in the sand.

A graveyard of wagons, left undestroyed because their destruction would send up a pillar of smoke that might be seen.

And horses. The bleaching bones of some, the half-decayed carcasses of others. The fresher, bloated shapes of those that had belonged to Sam and his brother Claude. It was these that had drawn the vultures. It was these over which the ugly carrion eaters were quarreling now.

Sam rode down the gentle slope into the bowl. He rode to the wagons that had so recently been loaded high with goods. The buzzards rose, flapping noisily, to resume their lazy circling overhead. They threw ghoulish shadows on the ground.

Sam felt cold in spite of the lingering heat of the day. A gruesome place, graveyard of more than wagons and the horses and mules that had drawn them here.

The seven wagons were empty now. Their goods had been transferred to other wagons and hauled away.

Where, he had no idea. Perhaps westward to the California coast. Perhaps southward into Mexico.

He would trail them if he could. If he could not, he would come back here. And wait. Those he sought would return. The number of dead wagons in this heat-baked graveyard would have to grow. And when they did return. . . .

He mounted and slowly circled the awful place, searching the ground for trail.

It was faint, fainter than the trail he had followed here. But he found it and rode out following it. When he had gone half a mile and had found the trail again, he stopped, taking a bearing from his starting point to where he stood and on to a carefully marked point on the distant, shimmering horizon.

The trail would be gone tomorrow. The point he had marked so well in his mind would not. When he reached it, perhaps he would find the trail again.

II

Until darkness halted him, he rode undeviatingly toward the marked point on the horizon. It was indelibly reproduced in his mind, so clearly that all during the night he rode toward it unerringly in his dreams.

He woke several times, sweating. His mouth was dry as cotton. His horse fidgeted uneasily where he was picketed nearby.

In the morning, Sam again poured water from the canteen into his hat and let the horse drink. Then he drained the few remaining drops into his own dry mouth.

Water had to be found, and soon. Else he and the horse would be added to the list of victims in the raid. They would die out here with vengeance unattained.

He dismounted and led the horse. Best to stay with this route he knew. The thieves had traveled it with their stolen goods. They had to have water eventually for their teams and for themselves. There had to be water some place along their route.

The land began to climb at noon of the second day, although the point of land he had marked in his mind still beckoned maddeningly from the distance. He climbed all through the afternoon, slowly, on foot, without once seeing the trail he sought.

He was gaunt and covered with fine gray dust. His beard was reddish against his dust-grayed cheeks. His eyes were red and rimmed with mud formed by moisture from his eyes and the unrelenting dust.

Sun reflecting up from the gleaming bed of the lake had burned his skin, and his face and throat were fiery red. But his eyes remained the same, chill blue, narrowed and hard as bits of stone. There was hate in those eyes, and outrage that did not fade, and the iron determination of a man who will have his way.

As the land rose, it became rockier. Now there was thin, dry grass upon the ground, a little feed for his gaunted horse. In the distance, on the rocky hills toward which he rode, he could see the grayish shadow that indicated cedars or piñon pine.

Water. He must have it soon or die. His tongue was swelling. His lips were cracked and bleeding. Weakness was growing in his strong, gaunt body, and he stumbled often now as he walked along.

He watched the ground for tracks of animals that lived in this dry land. He watched for birds, and noted the direction of their flight. Toward the rock-strewn hills. And he knew water was ahead.

He found it at nightfall, a damp spot in a dry stream. He dug with the broad-bladed knife after securely tying his horse, and, when he had gone down a foot, water began to seep slowly into the hole.

He splashed the muddy stuff into his mouth and licked greedily at his lips. He moistened his mouth again, then waited for the hole to fill.

When several inches stood in it, he led the horse to it, let him briefly drink, then hauled him forcibly away. He tied the horse, then flopped face down and drank himself.

Alternately after that he watered the horse and drank himself until both had their fill. He let the water clear, filled his canteen. Hungry, he picketed his horse and camped there for the night.

He slept in an exhausted stupor until the sun was high. And drank again, watered the horse, and at last went on. He had made it through. Hunger he could endure until he could kill some game.

He reached the spot he had marked in his mind that afternoon, and, after marking another farther on, he cast back and forth a mile to each side of it looking for trail. He found nothing.

That afternoon he rode down into a brushy ravine, surprised a deer, and killed it with a single shot from his revolver. He dismounted, tied his horse, bled and gutted the deer, and hung it up to cool. He ate for the first time that night, ate until he was gorged and slightly sick. He held it down, and in the morning felt strong again, and hungry, and alive.

But the mind sickness engendered by the

slaughter of the teamsters, by the sight of that gruesome graveyard of wagons, remained with him.

On again in the same direction. He knew he had lost the trail. He knew his chances of finding it again were slim.

But he also knew that, having headed in this direction, the thieves must have a destination in mind not too many days from the place they had transferred the freight.

Occasionally this day, he saw cattle, the tracks of a shod horse, those of the iron-tired wheels of buggy or buckboard. And from these signs he knew he was approaching a town.

Dry and barren country, this. A land guarded by brooding sentinels of gigantic mesas in the distance. Nearer were low and rock-strewn hills upon which the only trees were gnarled cedars and piñon pine, the only grass thin spears growing in the shelter of sagebrush sometimes as high as a mounted man's head. He camped in this high brush and the following morning reached the town.

It squatted untidily at the foot of an entirely bare and blackish mound of some kind of volcanic rock. An unplanned town, whose streets were crooked and narrow. But a town that, even from here, had an unmistakable look of prosperity about it.

He stared down at it. He had come to kill, and

kill he would before he left. He touched heels to his gaunted horse's sides and rode on down the slope.

There was a roadside sign at the edge of town.

Welcome to Los Finados
Pop. 247

Los Finados. Sam Duke's mouth twisted. He knew a little Spanish, picked up from a teamster during the long trek West. He knew the meaning of Los Finados. It meant The Dead.

At the upper edge of town he entered a street of homes, around some of which an attempt had been made to grow grass and gardens. Mostly the attempts had failed. Grass was spotty and dry and brown. The only flowers that grew were hardy varieties that required little water to thrive. But picket fences marked the confines of the yards. And for the most part the homes were well cared for and a few were freshly painted. Paint had been part of the cargo Sam's wagons had carried. But this was not that fresh.

He rode on, to enter the business street, wider and straighter than the rest. Downstreet, in the center, there was a well and pump and water trough. He rode directly to it and stopped to let his dry horse drink.

What few pedestrians were on the street stared at him. A rider went by with a furtive glance, a cold, set face, and only silence for Sam's curt nod.

Two loafers on the porch of the mercantile store puffed their pipes and stared at him steadily through the smoke.

A feeling in the streets—of hostility—of suspicion—of menace. Or was it himself, his own hostility, suspicion, and menace sensed and reflected back at him by the people of the town? He didn't know and didn't care. He was angry again, thinking that there were no main roads going through this town, nothing to explain its quite evident prosperity, unless. . . . His mouth firmed out. He felt like a fly with a foot in a spider web. If he struggled, he would become hopelessly enmeshed.

He lifted his horse's head and turned down-street toward the towering livery barn. Somewhere beyond he could hear the whine of a sawmill as the saw bit into another log.

The doors of the livery barn were open so he rode inside before he swung down from his horse. He batted dust from his pants and suddenly realized that whoever saw him, whoever had seen him, knew from whence he came. Beyond the town was high country. The dust on his clothes proclaimed he had not come from there but from the desert on the other side. And so, with their guilty secrets in their minds, those he sought would look upon him with suspicion and distrust. Perhaps by this he could pick them out.

A man shuffled toward him from the dim recesses of the stable, a man who glanced once at his face, then looked down at the floor again.

Sam said: "Grain him. And feed him good."

The man nodded without meeting Sam's eyes or even looking at him. He was shorter than Sam by several inches and older by ten years. His hair, showing beneath his tipped-back hat, was both gray and thin. There was a bitter cast about the lines in his face, an anger concealed and tempered by something like resignation.

Sam stared toward the rear of the stable. A breeze had eased open the big rear doors and through them, in the yard behind the place, he could see several big freight wagons.

He said: "Freight line, huh?"

The man glanced up at him. His eyes were blue like Sam's own, but there the resemblance ended. He didn't reply.

Sam asked: "Yours?"

The man shook his head. "I stable the horses an' mules is all."

Sam walked back along the alleyway between the stalls. He stepped outside at the rear of the long building.

There were fifteen heavy wagons in the yard. There were almost a hundred head of big, heavy horses and mules in the corral. Sam walked to one of the wagons and looked inside.

No dust on the wagon bed. But dust aplenty on

wheels and hubs. Desert dust. The same dust he had batted off his dusty pants.

He turned to find the stableman standing at his side. The man was watching him. Just watching him, with no expression in his eyes.

A warning broke in Sam's mind. He wanted to ask the man who owned the freight line but he had already exhibited too much interest in it. He had already excited suspicion. The silence in the man's eyes told him that.

He stifled both anger and eagerness. If he gave himself away, he'd be dead within an hour's time. He said: "Horse played out and I'm damn' near broke. But I know freighting."

The man's expression didn't change. Sam turned and walked through the stable and out into the sun-washed street.

There was a thinness about the air at this altitude, and the heat here was not the deadly, oppressive heat of the desert.

It was obvious to Sam that strangers were a rarity here. Too much furtive attention was paid to him. There was none of the easy, almost disinterested acceptance he had found in other towns. These people were very much interested in him. And very curious. Yet hostile, too.

Why? What reason did they have for distrusting him? Did the whole town share the guilty secret of the few he sought?

He shoved that thought aside. It was too

unlikely. No. This was simply a clannish, isolated town where strangers were customarily looked upon with distrust.

Standing there, his face darkened, he was reasonably sure that the wagons he had seen behind the livery barn were the ones he had followed from the graveyard of wagons in that dry lakebed. The dust was the same, and, while that was not necessarily conclusive, it was enough for a start.

Follow, then, the goods they had hauled to this place. His eyes went to the mercantile store two blocks up the street. It was the largest one in town, probably the only one. The stolen goods had to end up there.

The freight line operator had to be in on it along with his teamsters who had done the killing and stolen Sam's wagons and teams. The owner of the mercantile had to be in on it, too, else he would not accept a load of assorted goods he had not ordered specifically but must take as a pig in a poke.

How many others were in it, too? The stable-man? He profited by stabling the big draft animals and storing the wagons. He could hardly fail to know what was going on.

Sam felt as though he were walking through brush infested with rattlesnakes. He couldn't see them but they might strike him at any time.

Decisively he stepped down off the boardwalk

and crossed the dusty street diagonally toward a small, false-fronted building that bore the painted legend above its door: *Restaurant.* He opened the door and stepped inside.

There were three men at the counter. All three turned to stare at him. Then they looked away. Sam walked to the counter and sat down.

A girl came from the kitchen carrying three plates upon which flapjacks and side meat were piled. She glanced at him, then set the plates down before the other three.

She came along the counter and looked at him.

He said: "That looks pretty good. Bring me a plate of the same."

She seemed about to speak, then changed her mind. Silently she returned to the kitchen, a pretty girl of about twenty whose face and eyes held the same standoffish distrust he had seen in the eyes of the man.

III

Waiting, Sam Duke swiveled on his stool, fished a nearly empty sack of tobacco from his shirt pocket, and rolled himself a smoke. He had been rationing himself stingily because this was all he had, but there was no longer any need to deny himself.

He finished shaping it, licked the paper, sealed it, twisted the ends, and stuck it in his mouth. He looked at the nearest of the three. "Got a match? I seem to be out."

"Sure." The man withdrew several from his pocket and tossed them down the counter. Sam wiped one alight and touched it to the end of his cigarette. He drew the smoke deeply, lingeringly into his lungs.

He caught movement in the street and saw the stableman pass, heading toward the upper end of town. The man glanced toward the restaurant as he went by, but Sam doubted if he could see inside.

The glance made obvious what his errand was. Sam got up and wandered to the door. He watched the man go upstreet until he reached the hotel. Here he turned the corner and disappeared from sight.

Sam swung back toward the counter, to surprise the three watching him. He was getting edgy but he forced himself to smile. "Nice little town."

None of the three replied. They finished their breakfast, laid some money on the counter, and rose to leave. So far not a one had spoken to any of the others and this, too, was strange. It was as though they had nothing to say that they wanted Sam to hear.

The door closed behind them. Now they talked, but Sam couldn't hear their words. As they moved away, all three glanced back toward the restaurant.

The girl returned, carrying his plate. He said: "Some coffee, too."

She glanced toward the street before she looked at him. Then she put her full interest on him and it was the most open glance he had seen since his arrival here. She asked: "Passing through?"

He shrugged, studying her with interest equal to her own. She was not a tall girl, but neither was she small. She wore a fresh gingham gown, a hand-made checkered apron over it. Her sleeves were rolled up above her elbows to expose arms that were brown and strong. A wisp of hair curled across her forehead that was both flushed and slightly damp from the heat of the cooking stove.

A soft, full mouth and brown, honest eyes. Yet for all their honesty, they held something guarded in their depths. She said: "What do you mean by that? Yes? Or no?"

He shrugged again and a small grin touched his mouth. "My horse is played out. So'm I. I guess

I'll stay a little while. If that's all right with you."

"You getting smart with me, mister?"

"No, ma'am." He watched the flush grow in her cheeks, the sparkle grow in her eyes. "It's just that you didn't seem to want me staying."

"Why should I care what you do?"

His grin spread, softening all the harsh, angry lines of his face. He said softly: "Why don't I go out and come in again? Then we can start over."

For an instant her anger continued to grow. Then he detected a twinkle in her eyes, a twinkle that grew into a nice, warm smile. She laughed nervously. "Never mind. I won't ride you out on a rail if you really want to stay."

He returned her smile. "That's nice to know. The way the rest of the people look at me, I wonder if that isn't what they've got in mind."

His words brought the cloud back to her eyes and she turned away from him. She was gone several minutes, and, when she returned, she carried a steaming mug of coffee. There was no warmth in her eyes and her smile was gone. She said: "That will be twenty cents."

He nodded and laid it on the counter. She picked it up, opened a drawer, and dropped it in. She began to clean up after the three who had finished and gone.

Population two hundred and forty seven. And he wanted maybe twelve. Yet before he moved against a single one, even if he was sure, he had to know them all. He wasn't going to be satisfied with killing only one or two. He wanted them all, the ones who planned the raids as well as the ones who carried them out.

The feeling of being a fly with a foot in a spider's web returned, stronger than before. He knew he would be watched. Every movement he made, every word he spoke would be weighed and examined for hidden meaning. And if they guessed that he knew, realized that he was after them, then he'd die within minutes with a bullet in the back.

He got up, eyed the tobacco counter, and hesitated. He could buy his tobacco here, but if he did not, he would have an excuse for going to the mercantile store.

He took a toothpick from the whiskey glass on the counter and stuck it in his mouth. He went out and closed the door behind him, knowing the girl was watching him as he did.

For several minutes he stood idly before the restaurant, rolling the toothpick back and forth in his mouth. Upstreet there was the hotel, the mercantile store, a barbershop, and a dressmaker's shop. Downstreet there were three saloons and a separate, stone building with bars on the windows that could only be the jail.

A man got up from a bench in front of the jail and walked toward Sam. He stopped a dozen feet away.

"Sheriff wants to see you, mister."

"Later." There was something about the man's manner, an insolence that rubbed Sam Duke wrong.

"Now, mister. Right now."

Sam stared coldly at him. The man was thin, small, red-faced, and bowlegged. He wore his gun like Sam did and it gleamed with the care he gave it.

Sam looked long and hard into the other's eyes. He said deliberately: "You can go to hell."

The man's eyes narrowed. His face flushed dully with anger and his lips compressed. Tension came to him, tension that was matched by that growing in Sam Duke. If he let them get away with riding him now, he wouldn't have a chance. They'd push and push and they'd never let up at all.

The man reached up slowly and shoved aside the flap of his vest. Sam saw a deputy's badge on the pocket of his shirt. The man said: "Make it easy or make it hard. That's up to you."

Sam said implacably: "Later."

The man nodded reluctantly. "All right. I'll tell him."

Sam watched him turn and walk away. He waited until the man was a hundred feet away. Then he turned and headed uptown toward the mercantile.

Ahead of him, the stableman appeared at the

corner and headed toward him. He saw Sam, started visibly, then swung to cross the street. Sam moved to intercept him, abruptly changed his mind. He watched the stableman scurry, head down, along the street on the opposite side.

At the corner, Sam turned his head. There was only one place the stableman could have gone, that being a false-fronted store with a black and white sign over it reading: *Jules Hamaker. Freighting.*

His mouth made a sour smile. The sheriff was interested in him and he hadn't been in town an hour. Hamaker, the freighter, knew he was here. The stableman had been concerned enough to run to Hamaker, which meant he was in it, too.

They were identifying themselves as fast as they could, he thought wryly. And they didn't even know that he was after them.

The mercantile store was next to the three-story, yellow frame hotel. It had a porch with a rail around it. You had to climb five steps to reach the porch. Its double doors were open. There was a conglomeration of merchandise on the porch, carried there each morning, no doubt, to attract customers or to make more room within the store.

It smelled like all general merchandise stores do—of yard goods—of coffee—of leather and kerosene. There was a cracker barrel in the middle of the main aisle near the cast-iron stove. There was a desk in the rear with a counter running around it. The desk was littered with papers.

The tobacco counter was near the front and contained tobacco, revolvers, and knives. Behind it was a rack containing twenty or thirty rifles and shotguns. Sam stared closely at them. Part of his own load had been arms and powder. He and Claude had figured they would sell well in California.

A couple of loafers were sitting on boxes behind the cracker barrel. He could feel their stares, but when he swung his head, they quickly looked away.

He waited. After a while he heard steps in the long aisle behind the wall counter and, looking toward the sound, saw an aproned man coming toward him.

The man was big, with wide shoulders, a deep chest, and only the slightest suggestion of a paunch. He was dressed in a neat gray business suit, the coat of which had been removed. His sleeves, rolled part way to his elbows, showed muscular, hairy wrists and forearms. He wore gold-rimmed spectacles and a neatly clipped mustache. His hair, worn long, was gray, and carefully brushed back at his temples. A handsome man. A distinguished-looking man. A man Sam had come here to hate and kill.

The storekeeper looked up, saw Sam, and showed him startled surprise that he instantly controlled. "Hello. I didn't expect to see a stranger here. We see so few. What can I get for you?"

"Tobacco. A couple of sacks. And half a dozen good cigars."

The storekeeper put the tobacco on the counter top. He offered Sam a box of cigars and Sam took six. The man said: "I'm Dixon Fetters."

"Sam Duke." Sam wanted to refuse the proffered hand, decided it would be unwise, and reluctantly took it. The hand was damp and cool but its grip was strong. He dropped it as soon as he decently could.

He reached in his pocket, found a $20 gold piece, and dropped it on the counter. He took his change wordlessly and stuffed it into his pocket. He bit the end off one of the cigars and stuck it into his mouth.

Fetters was ready with a match, his eyes studying Sam closely, from his face to his dusty pants. "Up from the desert?"

Sam nodded.

"Heading over the flat tops?"

"Maybe."

The man wanted to probe more, Sam could tell. And he was becoming nervous. Sam could tell that, too. He lifted his eyes and looked directly into those of the storekeeper. Fetters lowered his glance first.

Sam turned and went to the door. He stepped outside, looked up and down the street, then lighted his cigar.

Anger was growing in him and mixed with it was a kind of nauseous disgust. Right now it looked as though everyone in town knew the source of the town's prosperity. It looked, too, as though everyone was, directly or indirectly, sharing it, closing their eyes to the fact that by so doing they became accomplices in the murder itself. But guilty about it all the same.

He puffed the cigar, savoring the taste absently, his mind on the things he saw and felt. The people, watching him furtively. The grapevine, that sometimes elusive frontier means of spreading news, in operation. Give them another thirty minutes and all two hundred and forty seven in the town would know that he was here.

Action was beginning down in front of the jail. Three men emerged, talked together briefly, then came up the street abreast.

Something tightened around Sam Duke's stomach like a convulsive hand. Little tremors touched his hands. His eyes became like winter ice and the lines of his face turned hard. Right now it began. They meant to test the temper of the steel. And if they found it wanting, if they found it weak. . . .

He stepped down off the porch of Fetters's Mercantile and took an indolent stance, spread-legged, in the street. He waited easily, puffing on his cigar.

IV

One of the three was the small and red-faced man who had earlier told Sam the sheriff wanted him. He was on the right. A second, on the left, was big and dark, bearded and glowering. This one carried a double-barreled shotgun with both barrels sawed off until the whole gun was hardly more than two feet long. The third, the one in the center, Sam judged was the sheriff. A man with an outsize head, one that was not only overly large but was also oddly shaped. Wedge-shaped. The upper part above the eyes was rounded, the forehead smooth and pale. Below the eyes it tapered past hollow cheeks, slanting jaws, to a sharply pointed chin. A small-brimmed black derby hat perched atop his head, slanted at a slightly rakish angle. A ridiculous-looking hat for so large a head. But while the hat looked ridiculous, Sam didn't smile. Because there were other things. . . .

The man's eyes, large, intelligent, and expressive, but cold as those of a fish. The mouth, like a thin gash in his pallid face. The hands, long, tapered, soft, but obviously strong as rawhide. And the gun—the way it was worn—the cutaway holster and the hand-polished look of the grips. A dangerous man. Sam had no doubt of that. A ruthless, merciless man, one to whom human life was no more important than any other kind.

The man smiled as he approached. The big one glowered fiercely at Sam. The small one's eyes mirrored satisfaction and triumph.

The sheriff extended a hand. "Karl Bosma, stranger. I'm sheriff here."

The smile was disarming, the extended hand a friendly gesture that Sam could not ignore in spite of the uneasy warning ringing in his mind. Against his better judgment, he stuck out his hand and clasped that of the sheriff.

He knew instantly that he had made a disastrous mistake. The sheriff's hand closed like steel around his own. Slightly off balance anyway by virtue of his extended hand, he felt himself yanked farther off balance by the sheriff's deliberate and powerful jerk.

He staggered forward, trying to free his hand. The deputy, the small and red-faced one, stuck out a foot, tripping him.

The sheriff released his hand as he fell and raised a knee. It connected with the side of Sam's jaw, its *crack* audible the length of the street.

Stunned, Sam sprawled in the dust. He doubled instinctively, to protect his belly and groin. From ground level he could see the worn, dusty boots of the big man only inches away from him. Waiting. Waiting for a lethal kick.

Instinct told him to roll away, but something in him demanded he ignore it. He rolled toward

the feet instead, convulsively and with consider-
able force.

The big man had no choice. He either had to
back away, fighting for balance, or fall.

He chose to back away. And Sam took the
opportunity to roll to hands and knees and begin
to rise.

He pushed against the ground with his hands
and came up into a half crouch. He heard the
taunting voice of the sheriff: "Go ahead, you son-
of-a-bitch! Pull your gun!"

His head swung. He saw the big man, who had
recovered, only a few feet away. He stared into the
gaping twin barrels of the ten-gauge and knew if
he touched his gun the charge from that scatter-
gun would cut his body in half.

He froze. The sheriff said smoothly: "That's
better. Rufus, give the shotgun to Dell."

The scrawny one, Dell, stepped to the big man
and took the shotgun without changing the point
of its aim. Sam knew what the three had in mind.
A beating. A savage, brutal beating that would
leave him half dead here in the dusty street. Then,
before he revived, they'd lash him to his saddle
and drive the horse at a gallop out of town.

His eyes went beyond the advancing form of
Rufus. He saw the faces of watchers on the other
side of the street. In those faces he saw many
things, among them fear—and shame. This Karl
Bosma, who wore the sheriff's star, ruled the

town by fear. And that explained some of the standoffish suspicion he had noticed in its inhabitants.

Rufus was no taller than Sam. But he was heavy as a bear. His shoulders were half again as wide as Sam's, his upper arms as thick as Sam's thighs. His chest was enormous, but even so was dwarfed by the belly beneath. And the legs—they seemed almost spindly by comparison but were strong enough and quick as those of a dancer.

Sam didn't wait for the man's attack. From the half crouch in which he had frozen at the sheriff's command, he launched himself forward like a runner at the sound of the gun. Straight at Rufus.

He felt the impact as his head struck the big man's mid-section. He heard the enormous grunt of expelled air. With the sour smell of that in his nostrils, he felt the man give before him and stumble back.

Something like a sledge descended on the back of his neck and would have snapped it had he not been falling away from it. That blow of Rufus's two clasped hands drove his face down into the dirt of the street, skidding, and he felt the burn as the skin scraped off his nose.

He fought his way up. His neck felt broken from the impact. Rufus had gone back a dozen feet and sat down. He was getting up, his face red with startled fury, his piggish eyes wicked as those of an infuriated boar.

From the corner of his eye, Sam saw Dell, the shotgun in his hands. The sheriff had retired to the building wall to watch. Rufus was coming now, gaining speed like a train on a steep downgrade. He had probably never lost a fight, else the sheriff would not have retired to the building wall. And, Sam thought, Rufus would not lose this one unless he could think of something soon. He could not defeat the almost unbelievable strength in this great bear of a man.

As before, he took the fight to Rufus instead of waiting for Rufus to bring it to him. He charged but, noticing that he would pass within ten feet of Dell, changed the direction of his charge at the proper moment, making it look as though he were avoiding the big man's countercharge.

Instead, he hit Dell with his body, bowling the man back a full twenty feet to fall skidding in the dust. The shotgun flew in the opposite direction, discharging as it fell. The charge of heavy shot tore into the building wall not ten feet from where the sheriff stood and the gun, propelled by its counter force, skidded along the street toward Sam.

He stooped and snatched it up. He thumbed back the hammer of the unfired barrel and drove the charge into the ground directly in front of the oncoming giant.

It didn't even slow him down. It was as though he never noticed it or the roar of sound that accompanied it. He had been hurt and probably he had seldom been hurt in a fight before.

Sam stood like a rock, waiting. He could draw his gun and kill Rufus with a single shot. But he knew that before he could swing the gun for a second shot, the sheriff's bullet would take him in the chest.

His breath came out in gusty grunts. His eyes were narrowed, his lips pulled slightly away from his teeth. His shirt was half torn off exposing his chest and one dusty shoulder beneath.

He side-stepped as Rufus reached him, thought for a breathless, panicky moment that he had not stepped far enough. Rufus's hand seized his shirt and ripped what remained of it from his back.

But Sam was swinging now, swinging the sawed-off shotgun as hard as he had ever swung anything in his life before. It struck Rufus on the neck, broke and wrapped itself around, its diminishing force and jagged edges tearing a bloody furrow in the big man's cheek. Sam still had the heated barrel in his hand, with the action and shattered stock at the other end. He followed and struck a second blow, this one landing directly on the top of Rufus's head. As the man came down, Sam raised a vicious knee, which connected underneath the giant's bearded chin.

The man fell, limp and monstrous and ugly in the dust. Sam swung around.

Dell lay spread-eagled in the street, his open,

empty eyes staring unseeingly at the sky. The sheriff stood six feet away from the building wall, frozen suddenly where he stood.

Panting, Sam said harshly: "All right, Sheriff. Pull your gun. And we'll find out right now whether I go or stay."

He watched the indecision in the sheriff's fish-cold eyes. He saw the threat and the promise there. And he knew that he had won.

He backed away, having more sense than to turn his back. He backed fifty yards up the middle of the street. And only then did he turn. Having done so, he walked to the entrance of the hotel and went inside.

The clerk was out of breath, obviously having just scurried across from the door where he had been watching the fight. Sam said: "I'll take a room. Send up some water for a bath."

"I'm sorry, sir, we're all filled up." The man's voice shook, so great was his fear. Fear of Sam and of what he might do. But a more deadly, lasting fear of Karl Bosma and his two murderous deputies.

Anger flared in Sam. It showed plainly in his face. The clerk glanced around like a cornered rabbit.

When Sam spoke, his voice was harsh but soft: "I could help myself."

The clerk's eyes pleaded silently. Suddenly Sam was filled with disgust—for this town and its people who lived with fear and had lost their will to fight. He said: "All right. Forget it." He turned and stamped angrily outside.

He stood on the hotel verandah, glaring at the town. Bosma had apparently revived his deputies, for the three were gone. So were the watchers who had witnessed the fight. There was an almost painful normality in the street as though everyone were trying hard to forget anything had happened.

Sam was startled when a woman's voice spoke from the far corner of the hotel verandah. "They're all filled up?"

He swung his head. She sat there alone in a wicker rocker, straight, her feet together in a way that was almost prim. Yet there was nothing prim about this woman.

Her hair was black, a rich black with highlights of brown rather than blue. Her skin was white, her eyes a startling shade of blue that reflected a color near that of turquoise, combining their own color with the green of her gown.

He said sourly—"They say they are."—and waited.

"You'll be leaving town?"

"Not just yet."

"Why not? This is not a hospitable town as you know by now."

He was conscious of his shredded shirt and naked chest, but he suddenly wanted to sit down.

123

There was something about this woman, a serenity that was like a cold drink on a hot day.

He walked to her and took the chair next to her. He said: "When I'm ready to leave, I'll leave. I never liked being pushed."

She studied him long and carefully until her scrutiny became embarrassing. He could see a pulse beating in her throat. At last she said, as though having come to some decision within herself: "You will need a place to stay."

His glance stirred with interest so strong that a flush briefly stained her cheeks.

"I am not offering what you think," she said with the faintest of smiles. "But I happen to have a vacant house."

He frowned, puzzled at his own feelings of disappointment. He supposed he had unconsciously set her apart in his mind from the others who were closing their eyes to the source of their prosperity and accepting it as though it were not born of murder and theft. Now it appeared she was no different from the rest. She was a woman of property and she surely must know the truth.

He waited.

"I am willing to rent it to you. Is ten dollars a month too much?"

He shook his head.

"You'll want to see it, of course."

He nodded.

She rose. "Mister Fetters has some very nice shirts for sale. Shall I meet you there?"

He grinned at her, watched her enter the hotel, then stepped down off the verandah to the walk. He went next door to Fetters's Mercantile and bought a shirt. Afterward, he went out back and washed up at the pump before putting it on. The woman who had offered to rent him a house was waiting for him in the front aisle of the store when he returned.

Fetters made a pretense of being busy arranging goods on a shelf, but Sam could tell he was listening avidly.

The woman gave him her hand, which was gloved in white. She smiled. "That's much better. I'm Grace Marr."

"And I'm Sam Duke."

Smiling, she turned and stepped out the door. Sam followed. She took his arm going off the steps and held onto it after they had reached the walk. There was a fragrance about her that Sam found disturbing.

He said frankly: "You puzzle me. People acted as though I carried some kind of plague when I first rode into town. They're more that way since I tangled with the sheriff. But you. . . ."

She smiled warmly up at him. Suddenly there was the faintest edge of bitterness in her smile, something not soft at all about her eyes. She did not enlighten him.

Again he was outspoken, for he wanted no favors done him that might have to be repaid. "Could it be you have a use for me?"

"Perhaps, Mister Duke. Perhaps. Are you a man who can be used?"

He looked straight into her eyes. "Only if it doesn't change the direction I'm traveling, Miss Marr. I don't intend to let anything do that."

"And what direction are you traveling?"

He grinned humorlessly at her. "I think the whole town would like to know the answer to that."

V

For two blocks they walked along in silence. He was conscious of Grace Marr's hand on his arm, of the disturbing fragrance he had noticed before.

It was already fairly obvious to him that Grace Marr was at odds with the town. Women they passed stared haughtily at her or ignored her altogether. And by the very act of offering to rent him a house she had demonstrated her defiance of the sheriff.

At the end of two blocks, she looked up at him soberly and asked pointblank: "Why are you here, Mister Duke?"

He shrugged. "No reason. I had a bad time of it down there on the desert. This happened to be the first town I hit, that's all."

She smiled with gentle tolerance. "I do not think so, Mister Duke."

He said: "Why should I lie? Who are you looking for, Miss Marr?"

She smiled again. "A man that can take on this town and win. I will help that man when he comes. I thought you might be him."

He hoped his expression, his words would not give him away. "Why must anyone take on the town, Miss Marr?"

Her eyes narrowed very briefly. "If you don't

already know, it will do no good to tell you now. At least I will rent you the house and you'll have a place to stay. When you decide you can trust me, come to me. I will help you all I can."

He smiled. "When I understand what you're hinting at, maybe I will come."

She turned in at a gate and stopped. "This is the house, Mister Duke."

He followed her up the graveled path and onto the porch. She opened the door without using a key and he followed her inside.

The air was musty, the air of a house that has been long unused. But it was pleasantly furnished.

She was taking off her white gloves. When she had finished that, she began to roll up her sleeves. He asked: "What are you doing?"

"I'm going to dust and sweep. I hadn't realized. . . . "

"No need for that. I can. . . . "

She faced him, hands on hips. She said seriously: "You sit down and rest, Mister Duke. After what you did to Rufus and Dell . . . well, you've earned a rest."

It kept coming out, he thought—her animosity toward the town, toward the men who ran the town. He asked impulsively: "What do you think of Dixon Fetters, Miss Marr?"

He caught the twist of her mouth, the contemptuous anger in her eyes before she hid them from him. Then, in full control, she said: "He is a successful and influential man."

"And a handsome man?"

"What are you trying to make me say, Mister Duke?"

"What your eyes and your mouth said when I first asked you about him. I want to know why you hate this town. Before I will ever trust you, you must first trust me."

She turned her back on him and busied herself with a broom. A cloud of dust rose.

But he enjoyed watching her. She was a lovely woman. Her body was strong and lithe in spite of the restriction placed upon it by the fashionable clothes she wore. He watched the play of muscles in her forearms. He watched her hips with frank interest when she bent with dustpan and broom. The color that stained her cheeks as she straightened told him she was fully aware of his regard. He grinned comfortably to himself.

She worked steadily for half an hour, and at the end of that time she had swept the entire small house, had made the bed, had dusted and polished the furniture. There was a smudge of dirt on her nose, another on her forehead. Her hair was disarranged and her gown was smudged. There was a faint shine of perspiration on her forehead and upper lip.

Sam asked abruptly: "You call yourself Miss Marr. By that I take it you're not married."

She glanced at him impudently. "You called me Miss Marr. I said Grace Marr. But I'm not married. Not now. I'm a widow."

His inclination was to remain silent, but he forced himself to ask: "Your husband. Is he . . . ?"

"He's dead, Mister Duke."

Her face was expressive by its very expressionlessness as she spoke. She had felt, perhaps still felt deeply about her husband and his death. And this might be Sam's clue.

He said: "My deepest sympathies, Miss Marr, *uh* Missus Marr. My own brother and parents . . . in the last year . . . I know just how you feel."

This brought close scrutiny from her, the closest yet. He said: "If you'd rather not talk about it. . . ." Then his jaw hardened and he said: "How did he die, Missus Marr?"

Now, very suddenly, all restraint and caution was gone from her. Her face became intense; her eyes turned angry and bitter. "He was murdered. Murdered by men who live right here in this town. I have waited . . . I will wait longer . . . but in the end I will have my revenge." She put her hands to her hair, smoothing it, fighting as she did it for her lost composure. At last she said almost coldly: "The rent is payable in advance, Mister Duke."

He fished a $10 gold piece from his pocket and gave it to her. She went to the door. Halfway through it, she turned. "I'm sorry I was so abrupt. I was upset. Please remember the things I have said."

"I'll remember them."

"I have rooms at the hotel."

He nodded. She hesitated still, seemed about to say something more. She changed her mind and went on out. He watched her go down the path to the street, turn there, and walk toward the business section of the town. She walked with her head high but her hurried pace betrayed her agitation.

Sam's inclination was to call her back. He wanted to trust her. But he remained motionless. He had known her less than an hour. She might be one of them, using the story of her murdered husband to draw him out. If he talked and if she was involved with them, his life wouldn't be worth a Confederate yellowback.

He closed the door and looked around the room. He was tired and near exhaustion. The ordeal of burying his brother and the other teamsters—the long pursuit across the desert—the thirst and hunger—lastly the fight with Rufus and Dell—all these had taken their toll.

He looked at the door. There was a lock on it and the key was on the inside. There was also a bolt.

He locked the door and went through the house to the kitchen door. He locked it similarly. He went from window to window, checking their fasteners. At last, satisfied, he went in and sat down on the edge of the bed to remove his boots.

With that done, he stretched out and stared at the ceiling.

But he found that he was wide-awake. The people of this town kept parading before his eyes. The enormity of the task he had set himself loomed in his mind.

He did, in no way, underestimate Bosma's deadliness. The man was shrewd, tough, ruthless. Sam had no doubt but what Bosma had already issued the order for his death.

Once they suspected him, and they must suspect him already, they must kill him immediately for their own protection. They couldn't let him stay, for in staying he might enlist help from the few in town who had their own axes to grind. Nor could they allow him to escape. He might return with help.

He forced his eyes to close and tried to sleep. His body was tense and he forced it to relax.

He awoke with a start and rolled off the bed, gun in hand by the time his feet touched the floor. He froze, listening.

The sun was high in the sky outside. The pattern it laid on the floor told him that. He had slept less than an hour.

But he was alert and sharp again. The sluggishness brought on by exhaustion was gone.

He pulled on his boots, rose, and walked to the

front of the house. He pulled aside the curtain and stared outside.

A man was hurrying down the street toward town, a man Sam had never seen before. He glanced over his shoulder once, seeming to look directly at Sam. Then he hurried on. A little man, dried-up, gaunt, dressed in a business suit and derby hat. A man wearing gold-rimmed spectacles and a small mustache. He had wakened Sam, probably by knocking on the door. But he had gone away before Sam answered it.

An agitated man. Sam wondered who he was and what he had wanted, coming here. Shrugging, he turned away, satisfaction touching his bleak blue eyes. They were coming to him already. And that meant he had worried them.

He lighted one of the cigars he had purchased before he bought the shirt. He sat down comfortably and blew thoughtful smoke rings at the ceiling.

If he had them worried, it meant they were afraid. But of what? Of a single man a single bullet could kill?

He shook his head. No. They were worried about outside interference. That was what they feared.

Before they killed him they had to know what had brought him here, whether he had drifted in by accident or if he represented the Army or some outside law enforcement agency.

Grace Marr might conceivably be trying to find

that out. He had a feeling he would see much of her in the days to come. The little, dried-up man who had knocked so timidly and then hurried away might have been after the same thing.

He smiled humorlessly to himself. Because their fear might make the impossible task he had set himself less impossible.

He stared down at his dusty, Army pants, at the darker streak along the seams where the yellow stripes had been. His smile widened, but his eyes stayed hard.

Bertram Pettigrew glanced back once at the house Grace Marr had rented to the newcomer. Then he scurried along toward the business section of the town.

He climbed the steps of Fetters's Mercantile and went inside, breathing hard. Fetters glanced up, and Pettigrew said: "Come down to the sheriff's office, Dixon."

Fetters nodded, his eyes immediately worried. Pettigrew went out, walked downstreet, and turned the corner toward the freighting office and warehouse halfway down the block.

Hamaker was out in back working, along with several of his men, at breaking open crates. Pettigrew stood in the doorway that separated office from warehouse and waited until Hamaker looked up. Then he gestured with a toss of his head.

Hamaker came toward him. Distaste showed in Pettigrew's eyes in spite of his effort to control it. Hamaker saw it and scowled.

He was a gross and smelly man who never shaved, seldom bathed, and never changed his clothes. A man with no perceptible desire for women and therefore with no pride in his appearance. A pig, thought Pettigrew. But a necessary pig. He doubted if another man in town, even the cold-blooded Bosma, had the stomach for the part of the job Jules Hamaker did.

Pettigrew said: "We'd better get together. Now. Down at Bosma's place. And for God's sake, hurry up with this last load. The way it is now . . . hell, it can be traced or recognized."

Hamaker growled: "By who, for Christ's sake? Don't be a damn' fool."

Pettigrew turned his back, saying: "Come on." He went out, with the sour smell of Hamaker rank in his pinched nostrils. A pig, he thought. A stupid, murderous pig.

Hamaker, Fetters, Bosma, himself. The four that ran this scheme. Hamaker got the merchandise. Fetters disposed of it. Bosma provided the fear that kept the people still—and Pettigrew, mayor of Los Finados and elected county judge, lent the enterprise his brains and the doubtful backing of the law.

He hurried along the street, turned the corner,

and continued downstreet until he reached the sheriff's office. He went inside.

Bosma and his two deputies were wrangling bitterly over the fight. Rufus looked subdued, Dell as wicked as a tormented rattler. Pettigrew said curtly: "Get them out of here."

Bosma nodded confirmation. Rufus scowled at the judge. Dell's eyes brightened.

Pettigrew said: "And tell them to let that stranger alone until I give the word."

Bosma nodded again. The two went out.

Bosma stared at the judge with his cold, intelligent eyes. "What the hell are you so steamed up about?"

"That stranger. Do you know who he is?"

"I know he's livin' on borrowed time."

Pettigrew stared at him contemptuously. "And suppose he was sent here? Do you think killing him will help?"

"Who'd send him?"

Pettigrew sighed. Bosma was intelligent, but sometimes he seemed incredibly stupid. He said patiently: "There are two hundred and forty seven people in this town. You've kept them frightened. But there could have been one . . . that was not afraid. Word could have gotten out."

Bosma snorted contemptuously. "The hell!"

"Then what's he doing here?"

Bosma shrugged, staring at Pettigrew closely. "Driftin' through. What else?"

"Then why did you try and rough him up?"

"He got smart with Dell."

Pettigrew said: "I thought you had more sense. If you'd left him alone, and if he was just a drifter, he'd have drifted on. Now he's riled. He's got a reason to stay. He's rented a house from Grace Marr, and, if I know her, he's paid a month in advance. And we don't know why he's here."

"I'll get it out of him."

"You let him alone until I give the word."

The door opened and Fetters and Hamaker came in together. Fetters immediately moved across the room, as far from the freighter as he could get. Pettigrew said: "Sit down all of you. We've got to decide what we're going to do."

VI

Except for Pettigrew, they all sat down. He stared at them for a moment and then he said: "What do you know about this drifter?"

Hamaker snorted: "Him? How the hell could we know anything? He just hit town this morning."

"You haven't heard anything?"

Hamaker growled: "I haven't even seen the bastard. Nick came over, though, right after he hit town. Said he was lookin' the wagons over pretty close."

"What else did Nick say?"

"That the guy was broke, or almost broke. He told Nick he knew the freightin' business."

"Anybody else know anything?"

Fetters said: "He isn't broke. He gave me a twenty dollar gold piece when he bought tobacco. Name's Duke. Sam Duke."

Pettigrew said: "And he would have paid Grace Marr in advance. That's the only way she rents."

"Then he lied when he said that he was broke." Fetters's voice contained a touch of fear.

"So he lied. Maybe it doesn't mean anything. Maybe he just didn't think he'd get a job very easy if people thought he had plenty of money."

Jules Hamaker said: "Why take chances? Get rid of him."

Pettigrew looked at Hamaker contemptuously.

"You may be a specialist in slaughtering teamsters, but murder isn't the answer to everything. Duke's wearing old Army pants. If the Army sent him here, he might be doing that just to throw us off."

Fetters said: "Or he could be a U.S. marshal."

Bosma said: "I'll take Rufus and Dell and we'll damn' soon find out what he is."

Pettigrew stared at him. He'd seen Bosma work often enough—on someone who was helpless and outnumbered. The man obviously enjoyed hurting people but he wasn't a fighter. Not unless the odds were right. He said contemptuously: "Like you found out a while ago?"

Bosma's face flushed, then turned white. His eyes were virulent.

Pettigrew said: "What do you think that little episode did to your prestige? The whole town saw Rufus and Dell whipped. They saw you back down. Could be somebody will take courage from it. You might have a little trouble scaring anybody for the next few days."

"I'll handle it, damn you!"

"All right then. Handle it!"

He looked around at the faces of the others. Bosma was furious. Fetters was scared. Hamaker seemed contemptuous of all the fuss. But, Pettigrew had to admit, he was worried himself. Anybody that could take on Bosma and Rufus and Dell and come out of it alive. . . . He said: "There's one way to handle this Duke that will

139

hold up later on in case someone does come here to find out what happened to him."

Fetters looked relieved.

Bosma asked: "What's that?"

"We'll frame him on a murder charge. We'll give him a trial and hang him." He stared hard at Bosma. "That's your department. But I want it to look good, understand? I don't want anything going wrong."

Bosma smiled.

It was an evil smile, thought Pettigrew. He wondered briefly if Bosma had any ideas of getting rid of him and taking over control. Probably he did. Probably he'd try getting rid of Pettigrew tomorrow if he thought he could make it stick. He said: "And clear your plan with me before you try it out."

Bosma only grunted.

Pettigrew stared around at the others with visible distaste. He said: "Just keep your heads and everything will be all right."

He went to the door, opened it, and stepped outside. He headed uptown. He'd have to talk to Duke, first chance he got. He was an expert at sizing up the character of a man, while diverting distrust from himself. It was why he'd gone to Grace Marr's house a while ago.

Now he'd wait and see what Sam Duke did. If Duke came to him, there was a good chance his suspicions of the man were right.

Dixon Fetters was the second to leave the sheriff's office. He went out hurriedly, soon after Pettigrew had left. Both Bosma and Hamaker made him uneasy. They were killers, the kind who liked their work, and they always made him feel that sooner or later one of them would kill him, too.

Something cold gnawed at his belly as he walked uptown. Things had gone too well the last couple of years. There had been no trouble, save for an occasional beating or killing within the town itself. And the money—it had rolled in, plenty for everybody.

Strange how prosperity, even though technically confined to a few, benefited even those it did not directly touch. The whole town was prosperous now, whereas two years ago it had been in danger of being abandoned.

The four—Pettigrew, Fetters, Bosma, and Hamaker—reaped most of the profits, but others shared. Bosma's two deputies received good salaries and spent it all. Hamaker's teamsters were well paid, and that, too, was spread out through the town. Fetters paid his own help well.

The saloons were prospering. So was every other business establishment in town. Even the ranchers benefited because Fetters was able to sell them goods at a price far below what they would have to pay for honest goods.

And they knew—the whole town knew the

source of its prosperity. Most of the townspeople had resigned themselves to accepting it, no questions asked. The few who dared ask questions had either been discouraged by brutal beatings at the hands of Bosma and his deputies, or were dead.

A shameful business, thought Fetters. He had paid an exorbitant price for the affluence that had been so important to him. He shook his head angrily. Everything in life had a price tag on it. And perhaps the highest priced article of all was labeled success. He had seen the price tag and had bought his success anyway. Now it was time to pay. Now and all the rest of the days of his life.

Passing the restaurant, he saw Vera Koenig standing in the doorway. He touched the brim of his hat and smiled. Her answering smile was warm, and young, and made Fetters feel about ten years younger himself. On impulse he stopped to talk.

They talked pleasantries for several moments but Fetters's mind was not on his words, or hers. He was trying to fathom the things she felt, things behind the meaningless words she said. For one thing, he thought, she would not take the big house at the upper end of town for granted as his wife Maggie did. And he was willing to bet she wouldn't spend her days trying to make him feel small, as Maggie did. And in bed? His eyes dropped to the line of her firm young breasts.

He raised his glance to her face again and found it flushed. Yet her eyes met his steadily and they were not displeased.

A strange excitement took hold of him. Perhaps success had rewards he had not fully explored yet. Perhaps there could be more to his life than Maggie's nagging voice and sour face.

He said suddenly: "Is the coffee hot?"

She nodded. "Would you like a cup?"

"I think I would. I just think I would." He followed her inside and sat down at one of the stools. It was getting close to noon but he had a little time yet. Time to explore the things that had so suddenly come into his head.

She got the coffee pot and poured him a cup, watching him oddly all the time. He said uncomfortably, not being used to this: "This is a pretty hard job for a girl as young and pretty as you."

She shrugged. "It's not so bad."

"Maybe. . . ." He swallowed, his throat feeling tight. He got a grip on himself and went on valiantly: "Maybe things could be made easier."

Her eyes widened, but they understood. "What do you mean, Mister Fetters?"

His face was damp with sweat. Then he plunged on. "Have you ever really looked at my wife, Miss Koenig? Or listened to her voice?"

She laughed. "Call me Vera, Mister Fetters."

"Then you call me Dix. In private, of course," he added hastily.

"All right."

It wasn't going to be hard after all. She understood his proposition and seemed willing to go along with it. His mind began to make feverish plans.

The door opened and one of Hamaker's teamsters came in. Fetters finished his coffee. He said: "I'll see you later, Vera."

"All right, Mister Fetters."

He went out. Maggie might get wind of what was going on after a while, he thought. But what the hell could she do about it? After all, he was one of the powers in this town. Even though his part of the job was a peaceful one, it was still important. Pettigrew and Bosma would back him up if Maggie kicked up a fuss.

That house of Grace Marr's—the one she'd just rented to the newcomer—would have been just right. But perhaps another could be found.

He realized that his hands were shaking, his stomach tied in a knot. But he found it oddly pleasant and the excitement that stirred him did not go away.

His head came up and a reckless light came into his eyes. Enough of being belittled and made to feel small and ineffectual. Right now he felt like a giant.

And why not? He was paying the price tag on

his success with guilt and remorse, with dreams of murdered teamsters even in the night. He had just as well have some of the benefits, too.

Jules Hamaker was last to leave. He shuffled out with a grunt at Bosma, and slammed the door behind. On the boardwalk just outside, he pulled pipe and tobacco pouch from his pocket, packed the pipe, and lighted it.

A bull of a man was Hamaker, an old, shaggy range bull, grossly fat but with strength that was still tremendous. He could lift three hundred and fifty pounds from the ground to the high bed of one of his freight wagons with scarcely a grunt of effort.

His eyes, sunken and all but hidden above his untrimmed, uncombed beard, were more nearly like the eyes of a boar than those of a bull. Small, shrewd, grasping, they brightened only at the thought of profit. Never at anything else.

Coal mines had been Jules Hamaker's life until he was fifteen. Poverty and unending, back-breaking toil had been all he knew. Hunger was a thing he fought but never quite forgot.

At fourteen, he killed a man for a piece of bread. And after that his lot began to improve.

It didn't matter how you killed, or who. All that mattered was that you filled your cramping belly or, later, your purse whose only purpose was to guarantee that your belly never cramped with hunger again.

The mines had beaten his brother Nick, had made a rabbit out of him. But they'd never beaten Jules. Nothing ever would now. He had $10,000 stashed away in cash.

Somehow or other, the more he got, the less comforting it seemed. $10,000 was a lot. Two years ago he'd have said it was enough. But now that he had it, it wasn't enough. No amount, no matter how large, would ever be enough.

His life wasn't bad, he thought. Killing didn't bother him the way it might bother other men. It was just a thing he had to do. Like butchering animals for meat. You got used to it. Bosma enjoyed it, he knew. But he never had.

He saw Fetters talking to Vera Koenig in front of the restaurant. That was something he wanted no part of. Women. Fetters was a god-damned fool to be standing there, simpering over that slip of a girl. As if he didn't have enough woman trouble at home.

If Maggie Fetters had been Jules's wife, she wouldn't have lasted a week. She'd open her sour, sharp mouth just once to him the way she did to Fetters, and she'd be dead.

Fetters went into the restaurant with Vera as Hamaker shuffled past the place. All this hubbub about the stranger was stupid, he thought. How could one man menace four of them who had fifteen or more men willing to do whatever they were told? The answer to that was simple. One man couldn't.

Pettigrew and Fetters were a pair of rabbits like his brother Nick. They jumped at shadows. It was really very simple anyway. If the stranger got too nosy, he could be killed.

He passed one of his teamsters heading for Vera Koenig's place and grunted at him as he passed. He turned the corner and headed for his office.

He was thinking comfortably of the hoard of cash beneath the floor underneath his desk. He'd finish uncrating this last shipment probably tomorrow. He'd haul it over to Fetters's place and be able to add another thousand to his hoard. And in a month or so, one or another of the men who were watching the roads that headed across the desert to the south of here would come in with news that another freight train was passing through. And Hamaker would strike again.

He shuffled heavily along until he reached his office. He opened the door and went inside. He sank into his creaking swivel chair, put his feet up on his desk, and puffed comfortably on his pipe. And his eyes went to the small trap door beneath the kneehole of his desk, where all his money was.

VII

Sam Duke, having walked downtown soon after wakening, watched the scattering four after the meeting at the sheriff's office from a chair in one corner of the hotel verandah. So engrossed in their thoughts were they that none of them noticed him sitting there as they passed.

He saw the worried look on Pettigrew's face, saw the flush of excitement that almost obscured the fear in Fetters's face. He noted Hamaker's unconcern.

Pettigrew was, he judged, the one who ran the show. Hamaker did the dirty work. Fetters peddled the stolen goods, and Bosma kept the town in line. A nice, neat arrangement. But not so neat it couldn't be destroyed.

He got up and stepped down off the hotel verandah to the walk. He turned the corner and headed for Hamaker's office.

When he noted the length of the building, he cut across the vacant lot between the rear of the hotel and the side of Hamaker's place. It was too long for an office alone. There must be a warehouse in the rear. And a warehouse could tell him lots of things. Things that would make him sure.

He realized how dangerous was the thing he did. But there was an edginess within himself, a demand for action and an end to fencing and delay.

A high board fence encircled the yard behind the warehouse. There were wide gates, obviously for the use of wagons, and they were ajar. He stepped cautiously inside.

A good time for snooping, he thought to himself. Hamaker was probably up front in the office. The other men, who worked for him, had probably gone home to dinner. He had seen one of them go into the restaurant.

At one side of the yard there was a shed containing a blacksmith's forge and shop. At the other side, leaning against the fence, were discarded wagons, parts, wheels, and steel tires. Beside the shed containing the forge there was a stack of lumber and a pile of iron and steel.

After ascertaining that both yard and shop were deserted, Sam crossed to the warehouse door, which was also ajar. Hamaker was certainly not afraid of discovery, he thought. But then Hamaker thought he had killed them all.

There was a pile of crates beside the rear door. He paused to stare at them. He felt his face flushing, felt the heat of anger rising in his body. Because he recognized those crates, the markings on them. There could be no doubt.

He wanted to storm inside and kill Hamaker right now. He wanted to confront the man and by killing him ease some of the outraged fury that had risen in his mind.

But if he did. . . . He shook his head almost imperceptibly. A shot would bring Bosma, his deputies, Hamaker's men. He'd be cornered in the warehouse, with but a small part of his vengeance achieved.

Hard as it was, he would have to wait. Hamaker's death wouldn't satisfy him. Not if the others lived on.

He heard someone coming through the warehouse. He glanced around anxiously, looking for a place to hide. But it was too late. The door slammed open and Hamaker stood, surprised and scowling, in the doorway. "What the hell do you want?"

"Mister Hamaker?" Sam's hand hung close, very close, to the grip of his gun.

"I'm Hamaker. Who the hell are you?"

"Sam Duke. I'm looking for a job."

"I got all the men I want. Do you always go around back doors lookin' for a job?"

Sam lied: "I tried the front. There was no one there."

He could see Hamaker turning that over in his mind, and saw the almost imperceptible way the man relaxed. Hamaker had decided it was possible for Sam to have come to the front door while he was still away, possible for him to walk around to the rear, arriving after all the men had left.

Hamaker said: "Get the hell out of here. And don't come snoopin' around again."

"Sure. But keep a civil tongue in your head when you talk to me."

Hamaker advanced a step, glowering. Sam stood his ground. He didn't want a fight with Hamaker right now but he hated the man too savagely to take his abuse. This was the one who had led the raid on Sam's wagons. This man's gun may have been the one that killed Claude.

Hamaker said: "You tangle with me and it won't be as easy as it was with Rufus."

Sam grinned humorlessly. "You think Rufus was easy? Try him sometime." The sour, rank smell of the freighter was in his nostrils, so strong they pinched together visibly.

But Hamaker changed his mind. He growled: "Get out of here."

"Sure." Sam backed off several steps watchfully before he turned. He crossed the yard to the back gate, half expecting a bullet in the back. It didn't come.

He knew now. He was sure. No longer would any doubt blur the course he had set himself. All he must do now was to find a way of killing the four before one of them killed him.

He crossed the vacant lot to the street, went on to the corner, and paused to shape a cigarette. He lighted it and drew smoke thoughtfully into his lungs. Nothing was to be gained by risking further contacts with the four. They were already suspicious enough of him. Now he needed time to think, and time to plan.

He walked upstreet and turned the corner toward the house he had rented from Grace Marr. He was not surprised to see her waiting for him on the porch, seated comfortably on the top step.

He went up the path and stood looking down at her.

She asked bluntly and without preamble: "Time is getting short, Mister Duke. Who are you and why are you here?"

He stared at her so steadily that she had difficulty meeting his eyes. And yet, so determinedly did she meet them in spite of her discomfort that he decided to trust her. He did need help. He was not yet ready for a showdown, for gunfire that would settle the issue before it stopped. Right now all the advantage was with those he sought to kill.

He said with equal bluntness: "I'm a survivor . . . of a wagon train they wiped out down on the desert. I'd gone ahead to locate water. When I got back, my brother and teamsters were dead. The wagons and teams were gone."

She must have suspected something like this but having it thrown at her so abruptly plainly startled her. Her voice was almost a whisper. "And you trailed them here?"

"Not exactly. I lost the trail. But I found their

152

wagon graveyard and I managed to get a direction bearing from there."

"How do you know . . . ?"

He interrupted harshly. "I know. The freight they stole from me is down in Hamaker's warehouse right now. There's a pile of crates in his yard that I recognized."

"And you've come for revenge."

"Yes."

"One man against the town."

He said implacably: "If that's the way it's got to be."

"You'll lose."

"Not if I can help it, Missus Marr. And not without taking some of them with me."

"One man can't fight an entire town."

He looked at her closely. "Is it the entire town, Missus Marr? Or is it just those four and the men who work for them?"

"Call me Grace, Sam. Please."

"All right, Grace." Watching her face, he could see that not all of her thoughts were concerned with the unholy four, their men, or even with the town. A part of her thoughts were personal, warm, concerned with Sam himself. She lowered her glance self-consciously before she said: "Right now it's the entire town. They're afraid, Sam. Terrible things have happened to the ones who weren't afraid, or to members of their families."

"Bosma?"

She nodded. After a pause she went on: "But if you make progress . . . if you can show the town Bosma and Hamaker and the others can be beaten . . . then you will find a few with courage enough to stand with you."

"And you?"

She glanced up, smiling softly. "I believe I have the courage now. I believe I have waited long enough."

A mixture, this woman. Softness in her, but softness encased in a cage of hardest steel. At war with herself, wanting revenge and hating, yet needing love as well.

He didn't speak, so she asked: "What plans have you made?"

He shrugged. "None. Until a few minutes ago I wasn't even sure . . . that the men I wanted were here. Now I am sure. And now I will make plans."

"What can I do to help?"

He said: "Tell me about the town. Tell me about the people. Tell me those that may help and those who will not. And tell me how your husband died."

She was silent for several moments, her face showing the pain of remembering. "He was big, like you. Several years older than I. A man, Sam. A man to make a woman's heart stand still."

Sam didn't speak. He watched her face.

"He took a train of freight wagons west. He was going to send for me as soon as he reached California. But he never got there. He disappeared."

"How did you know . . . ?"

"A letter reached me, mailed from this town. I don't know how it happened. Perhaps I never will. The letter may have been stuck to one of the crates and fell to the ground as the men unloaded them. Someone may have found it and mailed it as an act of defiance. It was written sometime before he died, I suppose, but never sent because he never reached a place from which it could be mailed."

Sam said: "And you came here because it was the only lead you had?"

"Yes. I would have asked questions in a normal way and they'd have known exactly who I was. But Bosma met the stage. He was very offensive and I didn't ask. The more I saw of the town, the less I felt like trusting anyone. You're the only one I've told."

"How long have you been here?"

"A little over a year."

"What explanation . . . ?"

She smiled faintly. "None was needed, Sam. I had a little money and invested it in houses like this one. Nobody asks questions of an investor, Sam. You'd be surprised." She smiled to herself, and then she said: "It has not been too hard for me. Except that all the women dislike me so. Perhaps because the men do not."

Sam grinned. Then he sobered and said: "They had a meeting just now down at Bosma's place. The four of them."

Her face mirrored concern. "Then they will try to kill you, one way or another. They will have decided that."

"Could be. Only they don't know who I am. They are probably wondering if someone sent me here. That will hold them back."

"It won't for long."

"Maybe not. Only I figure they're looking for a way to get rid of me that can be explained if necessary. They'll goad me into a fight. They'll figure some way to make it look good later on."

There was sudden, bleak despair in Grace's face. He knew she was thinking that however strong he was, he couldn't win. Not against these odds. Nor was he very sure himself. Looking down at her, he realized that for the first time he wanted to win and come away unscathed. Before, he hadn't cared.

VIII

Sam Duke's face was both grim and watchful as he slowly walked Grace Marr back to the hotel. Her hand was warm and light upon his arm. Her steps were shorter, faster than his. He tried to match his pace to hers in spite of the sense of urgency that kept prodding him.

The battle lines were drawn. He knew that the killers he sought were here and he knew who they were. They, in turn, knew he was after them although as yet they had no proof. A bullet or a fusillade of bullets could come slicing toward him at any time, without warning, without giving him a chance to save himself or fight back. Whoever happened to be with him—it wouldn't matter to Bosma and Hamaker if an innocent person, even a woman, was hurt or killed, so long as Sam was also killed.

His nervousness increased although the sun was bright, the day hot and dusty and still. Entering the main street, he stared closely at it for the first time, his eyes squinting against the glare. A dozen, two dozen places could conceal a hidden rifleman. The roofs of the store buildings with their high false fronts—the windows of vacant rooms and offices over a few that boasted second stories—passageways between them, narrow and dark even at this time of day and

littered with trash and high-piled tumbleweeds
—the windows of the hotel.

One thing and one thing only could be holding
them back, he thought. Fear. Fear that he was not
alone, that he was acting for someone other than
himself. They must think he was a lawman, perhaps
a deputy from the Territorial U.S. Marshal's
Office. They thought his unexplained and sudden
disappearance might bring others to Los Finados,
others who could not be so easily killed. A guilty
man lives with fear, he realized. If it were not so,
he would have been dead two hours after he
arrived in town.

With Grace Marr clinging lightly to his arm, he
reached the hotel without incident. He stopped.
She turned to face him and stared closely up at
him, a worried frown on her forehead. "Be
careful, Sam. Be very careful. I wouldn't want . . .
now. . . . Darn it, Sam, I like you. I don't want
anything to happen to you. I don't believe I could
stand it again."

"Again?"

"You're very much like him, Sam. You're the
first. . . ." She stopped, confused, and a flush
mounted to her cheeks. She laughed nervously
and said: "Let me go, Sam. I'm in quicksand
and everything I say makes me sink a little
deeper."

He grinned down at her, both pleased and
flattered, and some of the tension left him. She

turned and ran into the hotel and for several moments he stood there staring after her.

The sun was hot upon his back. A fly *buzzed* close to his head and he brushed absently at it with his hand. He became aware that he had not eaten and that it was long past noon. Still he did not move, instead waiting while he shaped and lighted a cigarette. With it dangling from his wide and thinned-out mouth, he turned toward Vera Koenig's place.

Except for Dixon Fetters, the place was deserted. Sam gave Fetters a long, level stare and felt a bitter kind of satisfaction when Fetters could not meet his eyes.

Vera watched the two anxiously, her expression puzzled. Fetters mumbled: "See you later, Vera." He got up, leaving the coffee before him untouched. He hurried to the door and went out without looking back.

Sam sat down at the counter on the stool Fetters had just vacated and shoved the coffee cup aside. "What's for dinner?" he asked.

"There's some roast beef left. Or you can have a steak."

"The roast beef will do. And coffee."

She hesitated, watching him, the worried, puzzled look still in her eyes. He wondered if it was possible she did not know what was going on. He wondered if she could be unaware of the murderous scheme in which Fetters was involved.

She turned away and went into the kitchen at the rear. Sam finished his cigarette deliberately and put it out in the ashtray on the counter.

After several moments she returned, carrying his plate and coffee cup. She put it down before him, got the pot, and filled the cup. He began to eat, conscious of her continuing scrutiny.

At last she said: "Mister Fetters is afraid of you. Why?"

Sam glanced up. "Afraid of me? Why should he be afraid of me? I've only met him a couple of times. I just hit town."

"He is, though. And I think you must know why."

Sam said unfeelingly: "You seem concerned, but I can't imagine why you should be. Fetters is a married man."

This brought a deep flush to her cheeks, a guilty evasiveness to her eyes. She said quickly: "There's nothing. . . ."

Sam said: "Yet. Is that what you were going to say?"

"I think you'd better leave."

Sam grinned sourly at her. "I haven't finished my meal. Besides, you started this. I didn't."

"You're a gunfighter. A hired killer. Someone sent you here."

"That's what they seem to think. And who am I to say they're wrong?"

"But why Mister Fetters? He's a perfectly respectable man."

Sam laughed harshly. "You're a mighty foolish girl if you believe that, if you can't see he's acting just like a man with a guilty conscience."

"Because of me? He hasn't . . . I mean I can't see why that concerns you."

Sam laughed again. "It's got nothing to do with you. Want some free advice? Stay clear of Fetters. He's living on borrowed time."

"Are you threatening him?"

Sam shrugged and returned his attention to his food. He didn't want to talk about Fetters any more. If he did, he'd say things he wasn't ready to say. Vera would tell Fetters and the storekeeper would, in turn, repeat what he had said to the others.

The girl might have pursued the subject, but she got no chance. The door opened and a man came in.

It was a man Sam had not seen before, a small, middle-aged, wiry man in a leather apron. There was some kind of stain on his hands, leather stain, Sam guessed. He must be either shoemaker or saddle maker. Maybe both.

Vera Koenig faced the man as he sat down. "Hello, Mister Champion. What can I get for you?"

He started violently at the sound of her voice, then licked his lips and said nervously: "Coffee, Vera. Coffee will do."

So far, the man hadn't looked at Sam. It was as

though Sam wasn't even there and this told Sam immediately that the man was very much aware of him.

Vera went to the kitchen for the coffee pot. As soon as she had disappeared, Champion said softly without turning his head: "I want to talk to you."

Sam swung around, irritated and not bothering to conceal his irritation. "What about? I'm not hard to talk to, friend, so go ahead."

"Not here. Not now. Later. I. . . ." He closed his mouth abruptly as Vera reappeared. He put cream and sugar into his coffee, sipped it appreciatively, then turned ostentatiously to Sam. He stuck out his hand. "I'm James Champion, stranger. I run the saddle and harness shop up the street a piece."

Sam's expression was not pleasant as he took the hand. He said: "Sam Duke. Make a good saddle, do you?"

Champion's expression brightened. "Man shouldn't toot his own horn too much. But I make a damn' good saddle even if I do say so myself. Best for a hundred miles around. Reasonable, too."

"Handle used harnesses, do you?"

Champion lost color and his eyes became evasive.

Sam said: "I asked you a question."

The man briefly glanced at him. His voice was

scarcely audible. "I handle used harness, mister. What harness maker doesn't?"

"Trade-ins, I suppose."

The man quickly glanced at the door. "Uhn-huh. Man buys new harness and wants to trade in his old. Some I just buy outright."

"Who from?"

Champion glanced at the door again—longingly this time. He tried to gulp his coffee and burned his mouth. He looked exceedingly uncomfortable for several long moments. At last he choked: "From anybody that wants to sell, I guess. Anything wrong with that?" He was defensive now. And scared.

Fresh anger touched Sam. Champion was typical of most of the townspeople or a situation like the present one could not exist in Los Finados or any place else. He might not be a killer himself. He might not approve of murder. But he was accepting the benefits from it just the same.

Sam said: "Suppose I had seven sets of harness and brought 'em in to you? Would you buy them? No questions asked?"

The man nodded dumbly and again tried to gulp the remainder of his coffee. He fished in his pocket for a coin. "I got to get going, Vera. See you later."

Sam said: "You haven't answered me."

The man stared at him desperately. "I want to talk to you. I've got to talk to you!"

"I doubt you can tell me anything I don't already know."

"Maybe not, but. . . ." Champion glanced warily at Vera. She was watching the by-play confusedly, not understanding their words but understanding very well the undercurrents of hatred and fear flowing between the two.

In spite of his anger, Sam felt brief pity for the frightened man. Champion wasn't equipped to deal with men like Bosma and Hamaker. Neither were the others in town. Unless they were organized and acted together in all things they were like sheep at the mercy of a pack of wolves. Besides, he hadn't come here to condemn a whole town. Only to revenge himself upon those responsible for his brother's and his teamsters' deaths. He got up and walked toward the window. He stared out into the street and said: "I'll talk to you. Any time you say."

Champion glanced quickly at Vera. He stepped close to Sam and whispered, his back to the counter: "Five o'clock. The saddle shop. I'll show you some saddles while we talk."

Sam nodded. Champion scurried to the door and through it. He stopped in the street to glance furtively up and down. Then, ducking his head, he hurried up the street.

Sam returned to the counter, picked up his fork and knife, and finished his meal. Vera's eyes were scared and her face was white.

She waited nervously while Sam finished his meal. She took his money and absently gave him his change. She watched him leave, both puzzled and afraid.

Outside in the street the day was warm, the sun bright. Yet there seemed to be an ominous chill in the air. There was an unpleasant feeling of premonition in Vera herself.

Perhaps, she reasoned, it was caused by the stranger, Duke. Perhaps it was caused by the fear that had been so noticeable in James Champion, or that which had been so obvious in Dixon Fetters.

Who was this Sam Duke, that he could so inspire fear in those he met? A hard man, certainly. One upon whom life had left its scars. A competent man, with steady eyes that seemed to look straight through flesh and blood until they reached the soul. A man who carried hatred in his heart, who was as cold as an executioner. . . .

A shiver traveled along Vera's spine. She knew that what she was contemplating was wrong. But she had been here in this restaurant for two years now and had yet to meet a man she could fall in love with or want to marry. Hamaker's teamsters came in here and some of them had propositions to offer, some even proposals. But there was something about Hamaker's teamsters. She didn't understand it, but they all gave her the shivers.

Yesterday she had suddenly decided that if she couldn't have marriage, she was going to take the next best thing. Fetters wanted her and plainly needed her. He was well-to-do and could give her the things she would never be able to earn for herself. And she was tired—tired of serving meals to dirty, sweaty men. Tired of waiting, too, of waiting for a man who might never come.

She stared at the closed door for a long time, her thoughts changing the expressions that fleetingly crossed her face. Something was building up— some trouble that would destroy her plans and those of Dixon Fetters, too. Plainly it was something dangerous or he would not have been so furtive about talking to Duke.

Her expression settled into one of decision. She reached for her shawl and, throwing it over her shoulders, went to the door.

She stepped quickly into the street, feeling almost furtive herself. She glanced up and down but saw neither Sam Duke nor Champion. Reassured, she headed upstreet toward Dixon Fetters's store.

He was busy with a customer, so she wandered to the rear of the long room to where the dress goods were. She examined the bolts of cloth absently, her mind anywhere but on the materials in her hands. She could hear his voice up front, deep, pleasantly polite, droning on and occasionally interrupted by the sharper, higher voice of the woman he was waiting on.

At last he came toward her and she studied his

face as he did. There was a slight shine of perspiration on his forehead. His eyes were both glad to see her and nervous because she was here. She asked quickly, almost breathlessly: "Why are you afraid of that stranger? Has he come to . . . ? I mean, is he after you?"

Something guarded came into Fetters's eyes. "What makes you think that?"

"The way you act when he's around. You're afraid of him and it shows."

He laughed but there was neither humor nor sincerity in the sound. "You're talking nonsense. Why should I be afraid of him?"

"That's what I want to know. If he's dangerous to you, I want to help."

Abruptly Fetters's voice lowered almost to a whisper: "How would you like to get out of Los Finados, Vera? How would you like to go some place . . . ?" He stopped uncertainly.

Vera said: "Then you are afraid."

"Yes, damn it, yes! But I can't tell you why."

She took his hands in hers. He needed her. He was, in this moment, like a terrified boy. She said: "Tell me what to do, Dixon. I want to help."

"There's nothing you can do. There's nothing anyone can do."

She tried another tack. "Mister Champion was in a little while ago. He talked to Duke. He made an appointment to talk to him again at five o'clock."

She felt Fetters's hands jerk. He yanked them away, too late to conceal the effect her statement had on him. He said: "Thanks, Vera. You've helped a lot. Now go back to the restaurant and wait. Please."

She looked up at him uncertainly, feeling in this instant something closer to love than she had ever felt before. She said—"All right, Dixon."—and started toward the front of the store. After she had gone half a dozen steps, she stopped and turned her head. Her voice was scarcely more than a whisper: "Don't make me wait too long."

Any other time such a statement would have brought heated interest at once to his eyes. Now it did not. Both troubled and confused, she continued to the front of the store and went out into the street.

Dixon Fetters wasted no time after she had left. He snatched his hat from the coat tree near his desk and hurried to the back of the store. He went through the back room, piled high with goods, and out to the wagon dock at the rear. He glanced up and down, then stepped off the dock to the dusty alleyway.

He hurried along it, cut through the vacant lot just short of the sheriff's office, came up in front, and went inside.

Bosma was sitting at his desk, tilted comfortably back, his feet upon it. He was smoking a cigar and should have looked relaxed but he did not.

There was a small, worried frown upon his face.

He scowled at Fetters as the storekeeper came in. "What the hell do you want?"

"It's Champion. I just heard that he was talking to Duke. And at five o'clock he's going to talk some more. Duke's going to his shop."

Bosma's feet came off the desk. The frown disappeared from his face. He said: "Anything else?"

"Isn't that enough?"

"Yeah. I guess it is."

Fetters hesitated for several moments, looking at Bosma questioningly. Then, apparently deciding Bosma would take whatever action was necessary, he opened the door and stepped again into the street.

This time, he walked up the street, not bothering to cross the lot to the alley again. He glanced into the window of Vera's restaurant as he passed, but did not see her. Vaguely disappointed, he continued to his store and went inside.

There were tremors in his arms and hands. His legs felt weak. He wanted to run and keep running until all this was far behind.

He wished desperately he'd never gotten involved in this. But it was too late for such wishes now. He had a sudden, terrible feeling that it was too late for anything.

IX

After leaving Vera's place, Sam Duke walked slowly downstreet until he reached the first of the saloons. The doors were open, so he went inside, a bit tense and watchful, and took a place at the end of the bar from which spot he could see the entire room and all those in it.

After a first quick glance at him, the three men at the bar returned their attention to their drinks and renewed their conversation, although in a lower tone. The bartender, bald, bearded, and grossly fat, came waddling toward Sam.

Sam said—"Whiskey."—and the bartender reached to the backbar and picked up a bottle that he slid expertly to Sam. A glass followed it and Sam poured himself a drink.

A clock hanging behind the bar said it was 4:00 p.m. An hour to go before he was due at Champion's place. An hour to kill.

He tossed off the drink, liking the bite of it and the warmth it put into his throat and stomach. It had been a long time. He suddenly remembered the last drink he'd had—with his brother in a town several hundred miles east of here. His face settled almost imperceptibly and his eyes became a bit harder than they had been before.

He forced himself to think of other things because, when he thought of his brother and all those teamsters lying there murdered, a recklessness rose in him that was hard to control. He couldn't afford recklessness. He needed a cool, hard head if he was going to achieve his purpose here and come out of it alive.

Champion might be the opening wedge that would split the town, he thought. If Champion found his courage, others might find theirs, too. And with the backing of even a small part of the town's people, Sam's task would have a vastly better chance of success.

He poured another drink and tossed it off. He glanced at the clock behind the bar. It was 4:15.

Faintly, in distance, he heard a shout, immediately followed by something that sounded like a cry. The sounds were not repeated, and, although he strained his ears, Sam heard nothing further.

But an odd uneasiness had been born in him. Violence smoldered in this town. Nothing happened but what possessed significance. These sounds might have been made for the purpose of drawing him out to where he could be killed. Or they could have resulted from more of Bosma's persuasion as he kept a recalcitrant townsman in line.

Sam got up immediately. He dropped half a dollar on the bar and swung toward the doors. Hurrying, he went outside, his hand never far from the grips of his gun.

Like a cougar emerging from a cage, he looked the street up and down, appraising it for danger to himself. Finding nothing in its appearance that seemed menacing, he turned uptown, walking fast.

He knew, suddenly, who had made those sounds. He knew, as surely as he had ever known anything. Champion had been ready to talk, and help, and somehow they had found it out.

He saw the crowd beginning to gather as he passed the hotel. He walked faster, still watchful, still very much aware that this could be a neatly baited trap. They could be waiting for him up there in front of Champion's saddle shop. And they might cut him down when he approached.

But no shots broke the stillness of the street as he drew near. There was nothing here but the gathering, frightened crowd. Nothing but the still, bloody, battered shape lying motionlessly in the dust.

The crowd was different from any crowd Sam had ever seen. They stood unmoving, staring at Champion with expressionless eyes and impassive faces. There was no talking among them; indeed no one even looked at anyone else. And they stood well back.

Sam shouldered his way roughly through. He crossed the cleared area to where Champion lay. He knelt beside the man and stared at the battered, pulpy face.

Champion wasn't dead. His chest rose and fell irregularly. But his mouth was smashed and bleeding; both his eyes were beginning to swell and would turn black. His nose appeared to be broken. One of his ears was torn and dangling.

Sickened, Sam slid his arms beneath the man's body and raised him up. Holding him, he stared bleakly at the crowd. "How long are you going to let them do this to you?" he asked. "When are some of you going to find guts enough to put a stop to it?"

Not a one of them would meet his eyes. They were like school children, tongue-lashed by the teacher. They stared at the ground at their feet. But they would not look up.

Disgustedly Sam turned and carried Champion into his shop. He let the man down onto his feet, still holding him up with an arm around his body and with the other arm swept the work table clear of the work that was scattered over it. Then he picked Champion up again and laid him there.

Bosma hadn't done this personally, he thought, but Bosma had given the order. This was Rufus's work. He thought of Champion trying to fight Rufus. That must have been like a mouse trying to fight the cat. He stared at Champion for only a moment, then turned toward the rear of the shop, looking for water and towels.

He found a bucket filled with clean, cold water, with a dipper beside it. He found a towel nearby that was almost clean. Carrying all three, he returned to where Champion lay.

He soaked the towel and laid it gently across Champion's face. The man stirred and a groan escaped his lips. Carefully Sam mopped the blood and dirt away.

Champion stirred some more, groaned several times, then opened his eyes. He looked up at Sam, flinched with terror, then, as he realized Sam was not Rufus, his eyes widened and he struggled to sit up. Sam held him down. "You stay put a minute."

Champion opened his battered mouth as though to speak, winced, and closed it quickly as cold air hit the stumps of his broken teeth. His face twisted with the pain.

Sam said: "I'll talk. You just nod your head."

Champion's eyes seemed to comprehend.

Sam said: "Rufus?"

Champion nodded.

Sam said: "They must have found out some way that I was going to talk to you this afternoon. I didn't tell 'em and neither did you. Only one other person knew. Vera. She went to Fetters and Fetters ran to Bosma with the news."

Champion's eyes stayed steadily on Sam's face. He looked entirely different with his face battered and swollen. If Sam hadn't known who he was, he wouldn't have recognized him at all.

He said: "You were going to tell me about

Bosma and Hamaker and Fetters and Pettigrew, weren't you?"

Champion hesitated for a long, long time. Then he closed his eyes. His face twisted, with fear or with pain, or perhaps with both.

Sam said harshly: "You needn't have bothered. I know everything you could have told me."

This brought Champion's eyes open instantly. At first they were unbelieving, but after they had studied Sam's face a moment, they lost this quality. He croaked: "Then this was all for nothing." He closed his mouth immediately, his face twisting again with the sharp pain of air on the stumps of his teeth.

Sam said: "If telling me about it was all you were going to do, it was for nothing. But if you were going to help. . . ."

Champion made no sign.

Sam asked: "Were you going to help?"

Champion lay motionlessly for a long, long time, his eyes tightly closed. At last he shook his head, but perhaps fearing Sam would not understand him, he opened his mouth and mumbled: "I don't know."

"Will you help now?"

Champion's eyes were momentarily incredulous. Then he shook his head violently.

"Will anybody? Or do they all like the money too damned well? Isn't there an ounce of honesty or guts in the whole stinking town?" He forced his anger to subside. When he spoke again, his voice was gentler and softer, too. "Want me to take you home?"

Champion shook his head. His eyes went to a door at the rear of the store. Sam walked to it and opened it, to find living quarters on the other side. Champion must be a bachelor, he guessed. He must live here alone.

He slid his arms under the man, picked him up, and carried him to the bed in the living quarters at the rear. He laid him down. "Is there a doctor in town?"

Champion shook his head.

"Who takes care of people who get hurt? A midwife?"

Again Champion shook his head. He opened his mouth and croaked: "Missus Marr."

"I'll get her," Sam said, and went out, closing the door behind. He went into the street. Part of the crowd had dispersed but eight or ten still lingered, gathered into little, silent groups.

Sam stared harshly at them, passed, and headed for the hotel. He stalked angrily across the lobby to the desk. "Which is Missus Marr's room?"

"Seven. End of the hall." The clerk seemed to begrudge even this small piece of information.

Sam swung silently and went up the stairs. He found Room 7 and knocked on the door.

It opened almost immediately. Grace Marr stood there, at first surprised, then pleased, then doubtful as she saw the expression on his face. "Come in, Sam."

He went in. It was the first time he had been in her room and he found it very pleasant, both to his senses of sight and smell. It was a woman's room, clean, frilly without being frivolous, and the air carried a light scent of perfume.

He said: "Champion has been mauled by Rufus. He says you take care of the people who get sick or hurt. Will you look at him?"

"Of course." She reached for a shawl and laid it around her shoulders. She went out, and Sam followed her, pulling the door closed behind him.

In silence they went to the stairs, down to the lobby, and out to the street. She walked lightly beside him, asking once: "Is he badly hurt?"

"Probably not. Looks like Rufus concentrated on his face. He's got some broken teeth, maybe a broken nose, and a couple of black eyes. He didn't fuss when I carried him in, so I doubt there are any broken bones."

She did not reply, but her eyes were angry and her mouth set.

In silence, then, they walked the rest of the way to Champion's shop and went inside. Sam waited in the shop part of the building while Grace went into the living quarters at the rear.

Occasionally he would hear her speak, her voice soft and sympathetic. He would sometimes hear the male drone of Champion's voice, or a sharp grunt of pain. He walked aimlessly around the shop, looking at Champion's work.

The man was a master leather craftsman, there was little doubt of that. Sam saw some of the most beautiful saddles he had ever seen. He saw a harness, too, hanging on a rack along the rear wall. Some of it he recognized—the mended places that he had fixed himself. After that, his face showed no change when he heard Champion's grunts of pain from the rooms at the rear.

Champion was typical of the people of Los Finados. He might deplore murder and theft, but he was not above profiting by it. Fear may have been his prime motivation in buying the stolen harness from Hamaker and Fetters, but greed was involved, too. And the fact remained that he had profited, along with Bosma, Pettigrew, and Fetters.

It seemed like a long time before Grace Marr came out, drying her hands on a towel. She said softly: "He's sleeping now. I'll come back after a while."

Sam nodded, looking at her approvingly. This was a lot of woman, he thought. A capable woman, in many ways. Yet her efficiency in no way detracted from her femininity. He said: "You're quite a woman. You have unsuspected talents that keep cropping up."

She smiled at him absently. Her eyes still smoldered with helpless anger and outrage over what Rufus had done to the saddle maker. She said: "Take me for a walk, Sam. If I don't get out of this town for a while. . . ."

Sam nodded. He could understand. He could sympathize with her feelings. He could imagine how frustrating her life here must have been, waiting, watching the things the four killers did to the town and its people, watching each new shipment of goods come in and realizing what it had cost in human life.

He said: "Sure. Come on."

She went out, and Sam pulled the door closed behind him. Grace headed for the creek that wound through the lower end of town and hugged the edges of it on the east. They left the houses and buildings behind and walked in the shade of willows and cottonwoods, and after a while Grace stopped and sat down on the whitened, bare trunk of a fallen tree.

The sun was setting beyond the town, staining the sky and the thin clouds it held a brilliant reddish gold. The air was growing pleasantly cool again after the heat of the day. Grace laughed nervously. "Sometimes, Sam, I just have to get away from it a little while. Sometimes I think I can't stand it another day. I think that hate has twisted me inside and that it will make me old and ugly before my time."

"I can't imagine anything doing that."

She gave him a grateful smile. "Thank you, Sam."

He watched the play of expression on her face, his eyes turning soft as he did. At last he said: "Things are moving fast. Too fast. They are scared or they wouldn't have sent Rufus to work Champion over. And no telling what they'll do when they're scared."

"What are you going to do?"

"I don't know yet. Are there any of the towns-people who might help?"

She frowned. "A few, I guess. I don't know for sure. After what happened to Mister Champion a while ago. . . ."

He said: "I'm going to need some help . . . all I can get, if I expect to do any good. Will you talk to a few of those you think might help?"

"Of course."

"And have them meet at my place as soon as it's dark."

"All right, Sam. I'll do my best."

"I know you will."

"I'd better get started, Sam." She stood up.

He stared down at her for several moments, studying her expression. Seeing what he wished to see, he put out his arms and closed her within them. He lowered his mouth to hers and kissed her long and hard.

He was startled at her response, which was

almost frantically eager. She broke away, murmuring: "Oh, Sam, it's been so long. A woman wasn't meant to live alone."

He reached for her again, suddenly no longer caring about the four he was after or about the town of Los Finados. For Sam, there was only Grace, and this soft evening, and this place where they were all alone.

She evaded him, laughing like a very young girl. "Not now, Sam. Not now. Wait a little."

"Wait, hell!" But he knew she was right and so followed her back toward town again. After a hundred yards or so she dropped back and took his arm, hugging it against her.

Dusk was settling rapidly over the land. The sky was gray, an almost ominous color after the brilliance of the setting sun.

She left him before they reached the main street of the town, and he watched her walk away, his emotions conflicting for the first time since he arrived.

He wanted to take her with him and leave before it was too late. He wanted a woman like this—had always wanted a woman like this. He could live out his life with her, sire her children, and raise them and want nothing else.

He had an ugly feeling—that if he did not take her now, she would be forever lost to him. Yet how could he leave—with his business here undone? How could he forget those bodies lying murdered on the ground, that wagon graveyard in the center of that blistering dry lakebed?

And how could she forget the murder of her husband, the vengeance for which she had waited so long and patiently? He doubted if she would leave with her husband unavenged.

No. Whatever happened, they would both have to stay and see it through. Even if it brought only disaster and death at the end.

X

Grace Marr was equally confused as she walked away from Sam. He had stirred fires in her that she had long thought dead. He had made her feel again, emotions softer than hatred and desire for vengeance. Not that she had lived exclusively with these corrosive compulsions. She had not. She had taken care of the town's sick and hurt as best she could. She had worked as the town's schoolteacher until the women of the town pressured their men into removing her from the job. But though her mind had never dwelt exclusively upon her need for revenge, her determination to achieve it had never wavered.

Now she frowned lightly as she went over, in her mind, the town's inhabitants, trying to select those most likely to possess the courage to help Sam Duke.

She turned in at a brown, frame house surrounded with a brown, dry lawn. She knocked at the door.

A woman answered, a woman who showed Grace instantly the edge of disapproval. But this was nothing new to Grace.

She asked: "Is your husband in, Missus Neidrach? I'd like to speak to him for a moment."

"What for? He ain't got any business with you."

183

"May I see him, Missus Neidrach?"

She thought for a moment the woman would slam the door in her face. But the deeper, inquiring voice of a man from farther back in the house brought a grudging—"Well, come in."—from the woman's disapproving mouth.

Smiling slightly to herself, Grace went in. She went into the parlor and beyond into the kitchen where she found Les Neidrach sitting at the kitchen table.

He stood up immediately, ill at ease and puzzled by her presence here. He was a huge, heavily-muscled man whose body proclaimed his profession. He was the town blacksmith.

His close-cropped hair was gray and coarse. His features were heavy, placid, impassive. His eyes, blue as the sky on a summer day, could be as hard as bits of stone or twinkling with good humor. Now they were neither, just neutral as he waited for Grace to say why she was here.

She said: "The stranger in town . . . have you seen him?"

Neidrach nodded.

"His name is Sam Duke." She wondered how much she dared tell about Sam. Certainly not that he was acting strictly on his own. If that got out, it would be Sam's death warrant. She said: "He is prepared to tackle the four who run this alone. The town has got to help."

Mrs. Neidrach said quickly: "You get out of

here, Missus Marr. You don't drag my Les into something that will get him killed."

Neidrach said: "Mama, I will decide. Now leave us, please."

"Leave you? With this hussy?" Her voice raised unpleasantly.

Neidrach's voice remained soft but a new edge appeared in it. He said: "Leave us. Now."

Grumbling, she left the room.

Neidrach said: "How can the town help?"

"I don't know. He will tell you that. If you agree to help, you are to go to his house as soon as it's dark. But if you do not help, you must keep this visit to yourself. And your wife must do the same."

Neidrach nodded ponderously. He frowned for several moments and at last he asked: "What do you think? Can Sam Duke win?"

A cloud touched her face briefly and went away. Her eyes were clear and honest. "I don't know, Mister Neidrach. I pray that he can. If I can only get someone to help."

"You are in love with him?"

"Yes."

"And you, Missus Marr? What is your stake in this?"

She smiled wearily. "I'm a widow, Mister Neidrach. They made me a widow."

Neidrach got up heavily. He walked to the window and peered unseeingly into the darkness outside. But when he turned, his face was set with decision. "I will help."

Grace felt suddenly weak. "Go to Sam's house as soon as it's dark."

"Yes."

Grace said: "And thank you. Thank you very much."

"I do it for me, for Neidrach. A man cannot fight an army by himself and he is a fool to try. But to join another army and fight . . . that is something else."

She went toward the front door, followed by Neidrach. She went silently out into the evening air and at the street paused and frowned in thought. Then, walking swiftly, she headed across town.

Occasionally, as she walked, she glanced behind, unable to quiet a feeling of vague uneasiness that had grown in her. She saw nothing, and so went on, but the uneasiness remained. It was a feeling—as though she were being watched—and she realized that it was quite possible that she was.

At the gate of Jack Shepherd's house she stopped and glanced quickly behind again. She saw nothing, and so went up the walk and twisted the bell on the big front door.

Here, too, it was a woman who answered the door and here, too, there was suspicion and dislike. But Grace went in and waited in the darkened parlor for Shepherd to appear.

There was sharp contrast between Shepherd and Neidrach, but she hoped their spirit was the same. Shepherd came in, tall, so thin he seemed emaciated. He was scarcely older than Neidrach but as weak of body as Neidrach was strong. He walked with a stoop and, although he was only forty-five, his body tottered and his hands shook as though with extreme age.

He peered at Grace through gold-rimmed spectacles and smiled a sad and gentle smile. "What brings you here, Missus Marr?"

"Help for Sam Duke, Mister Shepherd. This is the town's battle, too, not altogether Sam's."

"You know what they did to me for trying to fight them once?"

"I know." Like Champion, Shepherd had felt the brutal force of Rufus's fists and had almost died as a result. Now he was broken in body, an old man before his time. Yet there was something in his eyes.

He got no chance to go on. His wife came in from the hall where she had obviously been listening. Her face was pinched and hard, her eyes cold. "You get out of here, Grace Marr! You get out and leave us be! You know what they did to him before. I won't let it happen again. I won't! I'll go to them first . . . I'll give you away." Her voice rose hysterically. "Get out of here! Get out!"

Her body was shaking now even more

violently than that of her husband. Shepherd looked at her, compassion in his eyes. When he looked at Grace again, whatever consent might have been in his eyes before was gone. He said: "She's right. We have done enough." Shame touched his face as he uttered the words and his expression proclaimed his compulsion to make Grace understand. "I can't pass Rufus in the street but what something shrinks inside of me. I can't look him in the face. I would be no help to Sam Duke, Missus Marr. They would get hold of me again and I'd fall apart. I wish you hadn't come."

"So do I, Mister Shepherd. I'm sorry." She went out, knowing this battle was lost. Shepherd was an attorney, once successful and promising, who now lived entirely on what he had saved and on the pitifully small fees he got for handling property transfers and wills.

Neither Shepherd nor his wife went to the door with Grace. She went out and closed it behind her, hearing their voices, low-pitched and scared, from the parlor.

A town in the grip of terror. A town whose name fitted all too well. Los Finados. The dead.

Thoughtfully she walked down the street but at the corner whirled quickly and glanced behind into the deepening dusk. This time she was rewarded and saw the shape of a man duck quickly behind a tree.

Quiet terror possessed her. She went on, hurrying, and at the alley turned. Gathering up her skirts, she ran swiftly and quietly. She cut through a vacant lot, ran down another street, cut through another lot, backtracked, and came up on the same street she had just left, watchful and cautious. She positioned herself behind a tree and waited, breathing heavily.

Running hard, the man came along the street, started into the lot, and then stopped. He stood motionlessly for several minutes. Then he came up the street toward the tree behind which Grace was hidden.

He passed less than six feet away. Grace edged around the trunk, keeping it between the man and herself, scarcely daring to breathe.

Only when his footsteps began to die did she dare peep around it. He was now half a block away, disappearing into the dusk.

She waited several minutes more, than left the shelter of the tree trunk, and headed back along the way she had come. On the far edge of town, she approached a small shack in which a single light burned. She knocked softly.

The door opened and a very old man stood framed in it. His face brightened when he saw her and a mocking gleam came into his sharp, blue eyes. "I knowed if I waited you'd come to me, darlin'. Come in. Come in. I've a bottle of wine I've been savin' for this day."

Grace smiled. "Stop it, Mister Daley. You know. . . ."

"Call me Mike, darlin'." Grace went in and Daley closed the door behind her. He grinned broadly. "Tired of the young bucks, have you? Finally decided you can't live without me no more? Good. I'll get the wine."

Grace watched him smilingly as he went to the cupboard and got down a bottle of wine. He poured two glasses partly full and handed one to her. He raised his own glass. "To us, darlin'. To everlastin' happiness for a tired old man."

There was mockery and good humor in his joking, but there was more—a vein of seriousness that made her eyes brighten. She said: "I've come to ask you something."

"Anything, girl. You know that."

"There's a stranger in town." Quickly she told him about Sam Duke and about what Sam hoped to do. Almost fearfully she put her question: "Will you help?"

"Help? You know I will. Been too long since I was in a good fight. It will seem like old times." He stared at her, the mockery and humor fading from his eyes to leave them old and tired and disillusioned. "But will he want me, girl? I'm an old man for all I joke around with you. But I still can shoot a gun. I still can hit what I aim to hit."

"He'll want you, Mike."

She stayed several moments more and left with

some regret after telling Mike Daley to go to Sam's place and soon as it was dark enough to reach there unobserved.

Leaving, she felt a bitter pang of conscience, wondering if she wasn't talking these men into trouble that might result in their deaths. Bosma, Hamaker, Fetters, and Pettigrew had ruled this town by terror for two long years, killing or beating all who opposed their rule. Hamaker had nearly a dozen tough teamsters who were expert in the art of murder. She knew she had been observed and watched a while ago. What if every man she persuaded to help were beaten or murdered before he could reach Sam's house?

If that happened—oh, God—how could she ever live with herself again?

In darkness now virtually complete, she stopped and prayed silently. And then went on. She forced herself to think of Sam, of his strength, of the potential violence that so plainly lived in him. And thinking of him, her doubts began to fade. It almost seemed as though he was with her.

She visited half a dozen more houses in the next hour, receiving angry or outraged refusals at four, reluctant and fearful acceptances at the other two. Knowing she had done all she could, she turned toward the hotel.

Rufus lost Grace in the growing darkness when she ran from him. Later, he passed within six feet of her without realizing that he did. He wandered aimlessly and fruitlessly around town for almost an hour, trying to find her again. At last he returned to the sheriff's office.

Bosma was waiting for him, alone in the office. He stared hard at Rufus. "Well?"

"I lost her, Karl. She got a glimpse of me and took off like a scared doe. I never did find her again."

"You dumb bastard! Did she go back to the hotel?"

Rufus shrugged sheepishly. "I don't know. I didn't look."

"Where did she go while you were following her?"

"Neidrach's first. Then to Shepherd's."

Bosma scowled. "She's trying to get help for that damned Sam Duke. We ought to have killed him long ago."

"But Pettigrew said. . . ."

"I know what he said," Bosma snapped peevishly. "But he's wrong. Duke's no marshal's deputy."

Rufus said hopefully: "Want me to see Neidrach? And Shepherd?" There was something very ugly just now in Rufus's eyes.

"No. Not yet. Let's wait and see who else she stirs up. Maybe they all turned her down. If they've got any sense, they did."

"What if Duke does get the town to help?"

Bosma looked at him pityingly. "You think we can't handle it? There's you and me and Dell. There's Hamaker and he can round up close to a dozen men. This damned town doesn't dare fight back. They know what would happen if they did."

But the frown remained on Bosma's face, as though he doubted his own confident words.

Rufus continued to wait and at last Bosma said: "Go find Dell. Tell him to watch Duke's house. I want to know who goes there tonight so we can take care of them. You come back here and keep an eye on things. I'm going out for a while."

Rufus nodded and Bosma put on his hat and went out the door. Rufus followed him, pulling the door closed behind him. He shambled off in the direction of the saloons, farther down the street.

Bosma stood there thoughtfully for several moments. He supposed Pettigrew could be right about Sam Duke being a deputy U.S. marshal. If Duke was, then Pettigrew was also right about getting rid of him. It just wouldn't do if he dropped out of sight. His disappearance was bound to bring others to Los Finados to investigate. Nor did it seem reasonable that any one man would come nosing into something like this unless he had substantial backing some place.

Of one thing, Bosma was very sure. He and the others couldn't afford to let Duke get the upper hand. They didn't dare let the town organize behind him. The best thing, therefore, was to take the initiative right away. Terrorize everyone who even thought about helping Sam Duke. And a damned good place to start would be with the woman, Grace Marr.

She must think she was in love with Duke, thought Bosma, to have gone as far as she had in helping him. He began to grin slightly. He'd pay her a visit shortly, and, when he was through with her, she'd avoid Sam Duke like a plague. He'd put Rufus and Dell to calling on everyone who dared show up at Sam Duke's house. By morning they'd have changed their minds, or by God they'd all be dead. Tomorrow when the sun came up, Sam Duke was going to discover that he was all alone—even more so than the day he'd ridden into town. When that had been accomplished, then they could put their minds to pinning something on Duke. Like a killing that they could hang him for. It ought to be easy enough.

He turned and walked slowly toward the hotel. As he approached, he glanced up at the window he knew belonged to Grace Marr. There was a light in the room, so she must have gotten back.

He went across the hotel verandah, noticing the way the few sitting in the verandah chairs avoided looking at him.

It angered him vaguely, as it always had. However, although he hated admitting it, there was a desire in him to be accepted and liked. He never had been and he never would, he knew. There was something about him. . . .

Money and power were good substitutes, though, he thought. And he had both. He'd have more later when the territory had grown.

He crossed the lobby to the desk and nodded curtly at the clerk. He walked around behind the desk and helped himself to a handful of cigars. He tucked all except one into his vest pocket. He bit the end off and lighted it. He puffed luxuriously. Then he looked directly at the clerk. "I'm going up to Missus Marr's room. Don't disturb us, understand? No matter what you hear."

The man's face lost color. His glance dropped to the floor. He mumbled: "Yes, sir. Yes, sir, Mister Bosma."

Bosma glanced around the lobby again. It was deserted, for the night outside was pleasant and warm. He crossed the lobby and began to climb the stairs, a peculiarly mirthless grin growing on his face.

XI

In Grace Marr, as she nervously paced the floor of her room, was an ominous feeling of impending disaster. She stopped at the window and stared down into the street, in time to see Bosma disappear onto the verandah of the hotel.

Did they know, she wondered, who she had visited tonight and why? If they did know, the men who had agreed to help Sam were in deadly peril. And they probably did know. Rufus had followed her—to Neidrach's house and Shepherd's. If she had not lost him as she thought, he might have followed her to the others, too, hidden in darkness where he could not be seen. Bosma might know every one of the houses Grace had visited. Right now he might be preparing to retaliate.

She had been a fool—to think that any one man, even a man like Sam, could take on a combine like the one existing here and win. A few of the townsmen had agreed to help, but when it actually came to risking their necks and those of their families, they would probably back out. There had been a time tonight, and her face softened as she thought of it, when Sam Duke had been at the point of offering to take her away. He had been willing to forget vengeance in that moment, and she should have let him suggest it instead of running away from him.

Right now her own vengeance seemed unimportant when weighed against the loss of everything. Her husband was dead and nothing she could do would bring him back. Yet she knew that it had become a great deal more than simple vengeance to her. No longer did she wish to punish those responsible. Now she only wanted to stop them, so that they could not kill again, so that the town would be free from the state of paralyzed terror into which it had been forced.

She seemed to be waiting, and listening for something, but she did not know what it was. Puzzled and disturbed, she crossed the room to the door. Her hand went down, through no conscious volition, and turned the key in the lock.

She walked back to the window and stared again into the night. Her eyes took the direction in which the house she had rented to Sam lay, and fixed themselves as though pleading, imploring him to come to her.

She heard footsteps on the stairs and in the hall, and seemed to freeze. Never before had she heard the noises in the hall with more than a small part of her mind, but she did tonight. Tonight, for some reason unknown to her, that sound stirred in her an unexplainable dread. And perhaps justifiably so, for they paused immediately before her door.

She had no choice but to add up what she knew. She had just seen Bosma enter the hotel. Now there was a knocking on her door. It was soft at first, but increased impatiently in intensity when she failed to answer.

At last she called, her voice thin and small with fear: "Who is it?"

"Sheriff, ma'am. I want to talk to you."

"Wait for me in the lobby, Sheriff. I'll talk to you there."

"No, ma'am. I'll talk to you now. Open up."

"I'm not dressed. . . ."

"Put somethin' on. Are you going to open this door, or do I have to kick it open?"

Grace was silent for a long time. Her eyes went frantically to the window and for a moment she seriously considered jumping from it into the street. Anything seemed better than facing Bosma now. She knew he was worried about Sam, and probably furious that she had tried to get help for Sam. He was going to question her, and try to frighten her. She had seen Bosma work before— enough to know how brutal and merciless he was. He might beat her with his fists until she was virtually unrecognizable and nearly dead. Or he might submit her to indignities it would be impossible to forget for as long as she lived.

She could expect no help from anyone. No one in the street would interfere no matter how she screamed. Nor would hotel employees interfere. And Sam was too far away. Even if he had not been, she doubted if she would have called to him now. To do so would probably lead him into a trap that would mean certain death.

She spoke coldly, trying to conceal the terror in her voice: "You'll have to kick it down, Sheriff, because I'll never open it."

Fighting hysteria, fighting herself for control, she crossed the room to the door. If she stood immediately beside it, perhaps she could duck out and get away when Bosma forced it open and plunged into the room. It was her only chance. She would have to try. If she could reach the street—perhaps even in this town the men would not stand by and watch a woman mistreated in the middle of a public street.

He tried the doorknob first, rattling it, although he must have known it would be locked. Then, holding the knob in a turned position, he lunged against it, again and again.

It cracked and vibrated, but did not give. She had hoped it would, because breaking it open by lunging against it would have carried him halfway across the room when it finally gave way. Now he would stand back and kick, but she still had a chance. He would be off balance when the door lock broke and the door slammed open. In the instant he was, she might get past him into the hall.

Holding her breath, she waited. His first kick slammed against the door, thunderously loud. The lock rattled and something in the door itself cracked, but still it held.

Grace expelled her breath slowly. She drew a couple of long, shaky breaths. She was trembling violently from head to foot with her fear and with the awful suspense of waiting for the lock to break.

She was not an excessively fearful woman, either. If she had been, she would not have come out here alone looking for vengeance against the men who had killed her husband. She would not have stayed when she saw what they were, how strong and ruthless they were.

But something about Bosma. . . . There was something twisted in the man, something that delighted in inflicting pain. The more excruciating and damaging the pain, the greater his delight. She had seen Jack Shepherd after the beating Rufus had given him. She had listened to Shepherd's delirious ravings while his body was trying to mend. Bosma had stood by that day, lounging against a wall, while Rufus did the work. Directing it, his eyes bright and lusting and enjoying every blow. A shudder took Grace as she thought of it.

The second kick slammed against the door, twice as powerful and resounding as the first.

Why didn't someone come? Was it possible that Bosma could come into the hotel and do anything he wished, kick down doors, beat or mistreat anyone he chose, and no hand be raised to interfere?

She guessed it was. The third kick slammed against the door and this one was thunderous. The door slammed open, half torn from its hinges, and Bosma staggered against the jamb, all but blocking the doorway with his body.

Grace plunged toward it. Bosma saw her coming and tried to recover, but she struck him with her body and threw him farther off balance than he had been before. He staggered into the hall and Grace ducked past him, turning toward the stairs. She had made it! She was clear!

An instant later her heart plummeted. She tripped and fell, sprawling in the hall, her gown caught and held from behind.

He was on her like an animal, enraged and savagely efficient. The flat of his hand struck her twice on the side of the face, its unheeding force stunning her.

She fought clear somehow and got to her feet, only to be knocked against the wall, yanked back and flung into the room she had just left. Bosma slammed the partly shattered door behind him, and put his back to it.

His face was white, the lips drawn back from his teeth. He was panting softly from exertion. An ugly, promising light was in his eyes, one that made her shudder and turn her eyes away.

He said: "You've been making calls, Missus Marr. You called on Neidrach and Shepherd. Who else did you see?"

Grace didn't answer or look at him.

Bosma's voice remained soft, but it possessed a peculiar intensity. "Answer me, you little bitch!"

She looked at him and quickly looked away. She had been afraid before in her life—many times. But never like this. A kind of cold and paralyzing terror crept over her, freezing her, all but making her incapable of action. In this instant she thought she understood the hypnotic terror of a bird within reach of a hungry snake.

He crossed the room toward her, slowly, deliberately. She didn't want to look at his face for she knew the expression it held.

He stood over her for a long, long time. Motionless. Waiting. His voice was fiercely ugly. "Who else, damn you?"

She would scream the names at him in a moment. If she did, he would go away and not do what he was planning to do to her. She opened her mouth to speak, then shut it determinedly. No. What he did to her was not half what he would do to the ones who had promised help for Sam. If she gave him their names, it would be the equivalent of betraying them to be savagely beaten or murdered. They had trusted her. She must not betray that trust.

She did not see him move, but sensed his movement. She felt his hands at her neck. She heard a tearing noise and felt the pull as he ripped her dress from her back.

She tried to get away, clutching the shreds of it across her breasts. This time it was his fist that slammed against her forehead, nearly robbing her of consciousness. And his hands were rearing at her, ripping the clothes from her body as though he were a maniac.

She had promised herself that she would not scream, but she could not help it now. Her screams of terror and pain filled the room, spilled into the street before the hotel, flowed along the hall outside her room and down into the lobby below. But no hurrying footsteps pounded up the stairs and along the hall. In the street—in the lobby—in the other rooms there was only silence.

Down in the street those within earshot hurried away, not looking at each other. A few of them cursed softly and savagely to themselves. But none came to Grace's aid.

Nearly naked, clawed and bruised, Grace began to fight. Her strength could not match his, but for her size she was remarkably strong. She clawed and kicked. She fought to get away. She would make him beat her into unconsciousness. It was the only way he would get his way with her.

He made guttural, unintelligible animal sounds. He tried to pin her down, but she would not be pinned down. The fight between them went on, seeming to drag from minutes into hours.

What little patience he possessed suddenly disappeared. His clenched fist struck her on the point of the jaw and slammed her head back against the floor. Light faded to gray before her eyes, and then to black.

She could not have been unconscious more than a minute at most. When she could feel and see and understand again, she was lying on the floor and Bosma was standing up, his face bleeding from her fingernails but deathly white where it was not splotched with red. His eyes burned and his mouth was a thin, cruel line. His breath came raggedly from his flaring nostrils.

"Enough for now," he panted. "But god damn you, stay away from Sam Duke. If you see him again, I'll come back and finish what I just started with you."

Grace did not reply, nor look at him again after that one swift glance.

Although his voice was soft, he seemed to be screaming at her. "Answer me, you bitch! Do you understand?"

She knew she had won. All she must do was nod her head and he would go away.

She could not seem to do it. This was one of the men responsible for her husband's death. This was a man to be hated above all else in life. She looked up and met his burning eyes with an equally burning glance. "Next time you come through that door, I'll kill you."

Now it would begin again. Defiance such as she had shown him would enrage him beyond all chance of stopping him. But she didn't care. She wasn't going to surrender to this animal in any way.

Strangely enough, he did not attack again. Instead, he turned without another word and stalked from the room.

Grace quickly forced herself to her feet. She slammed the door and, panting with exertion, shoved the dresser in front of it to hold it shut.

She took the pitcher of cold water from the dresser and emptied it over her head. It revived her somewhat, but no amount of water would ever make her feel clean again. She found a towel and dried herself vigorously, as though she could rub away the feel of his hands on her. After that she found fresh clothes and hastily put them on.

She was trembling violently and near collapse from hysteria and nerves. She forced into herself some semblance of control. She forced herself to stop trembling and looked at her face in the mirror.

There was a blue and swelling bruise on her forehead, an abrasion on the point of her chin. Otherwise, her face was unmarked. The other marks, the scratches and bruises, wouldn't show.

Sam mustn't know about this. He must have no inkling of how bad it had really been. Because she knew instinctively what he would do if he were told. Whatever caution and good sense he possessed—whatever chance he had to win and live—would be flung away. Maddened, infuriated, he would attack them heedlessly, not caring how many or how strong they were. And he would be killed himself.

She had expected that, with Bosma gone, help would come belatedly to her door. She was wrong. Only silence touched her ears.

She sat down. Her knees were trembling so badly she could scarcely stand but her breathing was beginning to calm. She had to get away—from this town—from Bosma and the chance of another attack. Now. Tonight. If she had to walk, or crawl, she could not stay another hour here. If she left, then Sam would leave, too. He would come after her and find her and they both could live. In time, perhaps, this would be forgotten with other nightmares of the past.

Yet even as she told herself these things, her mind refused acceptance of them. She would not leave, for that was exactly what Bosma wanted. She would not ruin Sam's chances of achieving the vengeance for which he had risked so much. Nor would she surrender her chance to end the rein of terror in this town. She had waited too long to surrender meekly now.

Bosma was scared or he would not have attacked her and tried to terrorize her into giving him the names he wanted. Thank God she had not been weak enough to give them to him. Thank God for that!

Gradually she quieted. Her knees ceased to shake. The jumping feeling of nausea ceased to churn in her stomach. She wanted to shudder, but she resisted the compulsion, knowing it would only renew her hysteria.

Calmed, in possession of her faculties again, she got to her feet. Again she looked into the mirror. She would tell Sam that she'd had a fall. That would explain the bruise on her forehead and the abrasion on her chin.

She stared at the door. There was a feeling of safety in staying here even though she knew it was false. The attack had taken place right here in this room. There was safety nowhere in Los Finados as long as Bosma was in control of it.

Thought of going out, though, made her begin to tremble again. Angry with herself, she resolutely pushed the dresser from before the door and opened it.

The hall was deserted. She stepped out into it, but instead of going toward the lobby, she went the other way. There was a back stairway that opened onto the alley. Tonight she would use this one.

As quietly as she could, she went down the stairs and opened the alley door. She glanced right and left, then stepped outside. Immediately she began to walk uptown along the pitch-black alleyway.

Shadows startled her. Her trembling increased.

Dread all but obscured her thoughts. And then her anger began. Damn Bosma! He wasn't going to do this to her. He wasn't going to turn her to jelly inside, make her afraid of shadows, make her live in abject terror that he might renew his attack on her. That was what he had done to the town and he wasn't going to do it to her.

With anger heating her body, it was easier to walk alone through the threatening shadows of the night. She crossed the main street two blocks above the hotel and headed immediately for Sam's house. If she could just reach Sam. . . .

The light in the window was like a beacon to her. She ran the last few steps and knocked lightly on the door.

XII

All evening tension had been growing in Sam Duke. In some strange way, he knew that tonight would see an end to fencing, to sparring. Tonight the battle would begin, in earnest at last.

Grace was forcing the issue by trying to enlist aid for him. If she was successful, Bosma and Hamaker and the others would have no choice but to act. And when they did. . . .

How he came out would depend largely on luck and chance. He was badly outnumbered, and, technically at least, the law was on their side. On the surface it would seem a simple thing for them to dispose of him.

Yet fear would complicate their task. They were afraid he was not acting on his own. They feared he represented something they couldn't beat. But if he could insure continuance of their fear, and compound it, then they might get to fighting among themselves about what must be done. Some of them, Fetters and Pettigrew perhaps, might even run.

The knock on the door caught him unprepared. His hand went instantly to his gun and he crossed the room like a cat to blow out the lamp. In darkness he went to the door and opened it.

He realized suddenly how foolish he had been to sit in a lighted room with the shades up. Only the fact that they were unsure of who he was had saved him. Later, they wouldn't care who he was. Faced with the complete destruction of their scheme, fear of contingencies in the future would cease to hinder them.

He holstered his gun immediately when he saw Grace on the porch. The hammer made the slightest of *clicks* as he eased it down.

She came in—into his arms with an almost frantic eagerness. She was trembling violently. He kissed her, then tipped up her face with a hand beneath her chin. "What's the matter? What happened?"

"Nothing, Sam. Nothing. I'm just scared, I guess."

He released her and went around the room, pulling down the shades. Only when they were drawn, did he light the lamp again.

He swung to face her and instantly his face clouded with anger. "What happened to you? Did Bosma . . . ?"

She laughed nervously and not altogether convincingly. "Of course not. I fell, that's all. I stumbled on the stairs going to my room."

"If I thought. . . ."

"Sam, you can ask the clerk. He saw me fall. Now let me tell you what I've done." Quickly and breathlessly she told him of her calls and named the men who had promised to help. "They ought to be getting here any time."

"Anyone see you?"

She nodded reluctantly. "I'm afraid so. Rufus. He followed me until I realized he was watching me. Then I ran and gave him the slip."

"But he knows you were making calls. How many had you made before you lost him?"

"Two. On Neidrach and Shepherd. I'm sorry, Sam. I didn't know . . . at first. . . ."

"Forget it. They'll know soon enough anyway. They're probably watching this house right now."

There was a furtive knock on the door, and again Sam blew out the lamp before he answered it. Grace stood close behind him to identify the caller. She said softly: "It's Mister Neidrach, Sam."

Sam held the door while Neidrach came in. He closed it and re-lighted the lamp. Grace said: "Mister Duke . . . Mister Neidrach. He's the town's blacksmith, Sam."

Scarcely had Sam finished shaking Neidrach's enormous hand than he heard a second knock at the door. Again he blew out the lamp, and again opened the door in darkness. This time there were three men on the porch, men who Grace identified as Mike Daley, Jubal Jones, and Manuel Santos. They came in and, after the lamp had been lighted, shook hands with Sam.

Daley said immediately: "There's a skulker across the street, Mister Duke. Watching the house. Looked like that deputy, Dell."

Sam scowled. "If you recognized him, then he probably recognized you, too."

The statement increased the worried expressions on their faces. Sam glanced at Grace. "This all of them?"

"Yes."

"Only Dell doesn't know it is. So he won't leave for a while . . . until he's sure."

"What are you going to do?"

Sam glanced at the faces of the four. He said: "We'd all better get one thing straight right now. We won't beat Bosma and Hamaker and Fetters and Pettigrew by ordinary means. There's only one way to beat them and that's to be as ruthless as they are. Have you men got the stomachs for it?"

Daley was the only one to meet his eyes steadily. Neidrach stared at the floor, nodding uncertainly. Jones, a small, dried up man with the calloused, weather-beaten hands of a working-man, glanced toward the window. Santos, dark and wiry and tall, with hair graying at the temples, said: "We will have to."

Sam nodded. They weren't much, he thought, but they were all he was going to get. Perhaps, when the action started they would grow steadier. He said: "You know damned well what Dell will do as soon as he's sure nobody else is coming."

Nobody answered him.

He said: "And you know what will happen to

you tonight if Bosma finds out from Dell exactly who you are."

Now even Daley refused to meet his glance.

Sam said harshly: "There's only one thing to do and you all know what it is." Anger touched him briefly when they still remained silent, then it went away. He said: "Wait here for me. I'll be back as soon as I can." He turned toward the rear of the house, immediately ashamed of his anger. The problem was his, not theirs. If they helped him in the open battle that was sure to come, it would be enough. Grace called softly: "Sam, be careful."

He glanced around at her. Her eyes were soft, scared, yet holding an elusive quality that made him feel ten feet tall.

He eased out the back door after first closing the door between kitchen and parlor so that no light could leak through, and stood for a moment in the darkness.

This kind of thing was distasteful to him and he had never done anything like it before. But he couldn't risk a gunshot. He had no choice but to slip up on Dell and kill him, without mercy, in any soundless way he could.

Reluctant, he lingered yet a little longer, renewing memory in his mind to make the doing easier. He remembered the bodies lying on the ground where Hamaker and his teamsters had left them. He remembered the graveyard of freight wagons, each representing one or more men murdered in cold blood for the things that they possessed. He thought of Hamaker, and Bosma, and of Rufus and Dell and the things they had done to the people of this town. Had he known about Bosma's attack on Grace he would not have needed to refresh his memories. But he did not know.

His face grim, he moved out into the darkness of the yard. Walking all but soundlessly, he went down the alley to the street, here turning and going a block to the next alley, where he turned again. Going back in the direction he had come, his eyes were narrowed, his ears tuned to each small sound that broke the silence of the night.

From the main street of town he could hear the faint and all but inaudible *tinkle* of a saloon piano. Occasionally he would hear a voice raised, or a shout, and far on the other edge of town a dog was barking monotonously. Ahead there was nothing.

He kept his glance steadily upon the lighted windows of his own house, knowing that anyone between him and the house would be silhouetted against the light. But too many obstructions were in the way—trees—houses—fences—sheds.

He reached the rear of the house directly across the street from his own and stopped to listen again. The windows of this house were dark. He eased into the back yard and through the weeds as silently as he could, hoping that whoever might live here did not have a dog.

He reached the wall of the house and moved silently along beside it, as much of his attention on the ground he was covering as on possible hazards ahead.

Eventually, without making more than a small amount of noise, he reached the front of the house where he had an unobstructed view of the street. He had been gone nearly fifteen minutes and hoped Dell was still waiting and watching for later arrivals.

For what seemed an eternity he stood at the corner of the house, his eyes probing the shadows, particularly those surrounding trees and bushes on this side of the street. And at last he saw what he had been waiting to see. Brief movement, elusive and soon gone, but plain enough to someone watching for it.

Immediately he moved across the dry lawn, half afraid the rustling of the grass underfoot would betray his presence, half hoping that it would.

But he reached the tree toward which he was heading without giving himself away.

He stopped with the trunk of it between himself and the lounging Dell. Killing this way went against his grain but he knew of no other solution. If Dell carried what he knew to Bosma, not a one of the four across the street would escape a beating or worse tonight. Sam's chance of winning against the murderous four would be gone.

As he stepped around the tree, his foot came

down squarely upon a dead twig lying there. He may have put it there deliberately for he had seen the twig. Quite possibly it was not in him to murder without warning from behind.

In any event, the problem resolved itself. Dell whirled nervously, starting violently when he saw Sam standing so close to him.

His hand was like light, going for the gun hanging at his side. But Sam's was faster.

Sam's thumb failed to cock the hammer as his gun came up. Fisted in his hand, it swung with a chopping motion and the barrel struck Dell beside the jaw. Then with equal force he brought the long barrel slashing against the side of his neck.

Dell dropped like a steer stunned by a butcher's sledge, but Sam was in the grip of reflex now and could not stop. He was a fighting animal, savage, merciless, efficient. Twice more before Dell could hit the ground, Sam's gun slashed, and twice connected with Dell's head or neck.

Dell hit the ground soddenly and for an instant Sam stood over him, breathing hard. He hoped Dell was dead because he couldn't afford to let him live. He holstered his gun and knelt in the darkness beside the still form of Bosma's murderous deputy.

He put his hand lightly on Dell's chest. He could detect no rise and fall and so picked up the man's wrist and felt carefully for pulse. There was none.

He seized the deputy beneath the arms and hoisted him to his feet. Stooping slightly, he picked the body up slung across his right shoulder.

Walking strongly as though the weight were negligible, he crossed a vacant lot to the alley and on beyond to the main street of the town. He paused here for several moments while he carefully scanned the street. Then he crossed it, sidled between two buildings to the trash-littered rear of one of them. Here he put Dell down, arranging the body so that it would look as though he had died right here.

He returned quickly, again scanning the main street for danger to himself. He crossed it without being seen, and returned to the house where the others were waiting for him. He knocked lightly on the door, then opened it.

He said: "You can stop worrying about Dell. He's dead." Before they could reply, he added harshly: "There will be more killing . . . on one side or the other. Prepare yourselves for that. They've had two years to get a strangle hold on this town and somebody is sure to get hurt breaking it. But if you want it broken, it can be done. Do any of you know others that you can get to help?"

They all thought briefly, then nodded silently.

Sam asked: "How many?"

Each told him the names of others they felt sure would help.

Sam added up the total in his mind. With the four and himself, it came to eleven. He said: "All right. Go home. See the others, either tonight or first thing tomorrow morning. Get together what guns and ammunition you have. Don't slip around like thieves but try not to be seen. I'll let you know when I need you and what each one of you is to do. If you hear shooting, no matter what time of day or night, come running. Have you got that clear?"

They nodded uneasily. He could see that they dreaded separating, that they found comfort and courage in their numbers. Neidrach paused with his hand on the doorknob and asked with forced determination: "What's your stake in this, Duke?"

Sam knew the risk he took in revealing the fact that he was acting on his own. Yet he also knew how badly he needed the trust of these men upon whom he was depending for help. He said bluntly: "My brother and I had a wagon train. Hamaker slaughtered my brother and teamsters and stole the wagons. The goods we were hauling are down in Hamaker's warehouse right now. Before I leave this town I'm going to see every damned one of them lying dead. Does that answer you?"

Neidrach nodded.

Sam cautioned: "They can kill me pretty easily if they put their minds to it. The only thing that's holding them back is their fear that I might be a U.S. marshal's deputy and the hope that I may not know all the details of their scheme. If they find out I'm acting strictly on my own, I won't last longer than a snowball in hell."

Neidrach said: "We won't talk, Duke. You can count on that."

Sam nodded, and they all filed out. He didn't trust Neidrach's assurance, but under the circumstances he had done the only thing he could.

When they all had gone, Grace asked worriedly: "Sam, was that wise? If Rufus . . . ?"

Sam said: "They've got to trust me. And they won't if I hold out on them."

He had put his life in the hands of the four who had just left here. He could not leave it there for long. Nor could he afford to let the impending showdown be long delayed or the townsmen would lose the courage that had led them to promise help.

He must push the murderous four—put pressure on them—force them to act, and soon. It was the only way he could hope to win, and he must begin tonight.

Frowning, he tried to decide which of the four it would be wisest to begin with. Fetters was the weakest of the four, he thought. Fetters would do to start.

But right now there was Grace, looking up at him with fearful eyes, and right now they were alone.

XIII

Looking up at Sam, Grace knew suddenly how unimportant was the vengeance she had waited so long to achieve. His expression, usually harsh, was now very gentle as he stared down at her. Yet smoldering behind his eyes were fires that made her heart beat fast.

He said: "It ought to be over by this time tomorrow."

"That soon?" Her voice sounded breathless, frightened.

"Yes."

Her eyes clung to his almost desperately. Would he be alive and unhurt tomorrow night? Or would he . . . ? She turned her glance from his so that he would not guess her thoughts.

She thought of going back to the hotel alone and felt something shrink painfully within her chest. When Bosma found Dell's body, he would be out of his mind with rage. He'd strike out like a wounded rattler at anything within his reach.

She glanced up at Sam, a tiny smile touching the corners of her mouth. She wanted to stay here with him, she thought. Where Sam was concerned, there were no reservations and would never be. She'd go with him, stay with him, with or without marriage. The smile died and a prayer for his safety repeated itself again and again in her mind.

Sam asked softly: "What are you thinking?"

"How much I love you, Sam. Is it possible to fall so deeply in love so quickly?"

"It must be possible. I've done it myself."

She felt his hands touching her, burning her upper arms as he drew her close. She felt the hard, deep strength of his chest, the hungry bite of his fingers as they tightened around her arms.

She murmured reluctantly: "I've got to go back."

"Why?"

"Because I have to, Sam." She felt herself weakening. She wanted nothing more than to stay here with him tonight. If anything happened tomorrow, they would at least have had that much. But she didn't dare. If she stayed, he would see the bruises, the scratches now covered by her clothes. And if he saw those marks, he would forget whatever caution he possessed and whatever strategy he had planned. Forgetting, he would be killed.

His mouth was hungry, demanding, seeking hers. For an instant her arms tightened involuntarily around his neck and her body arched closely to him.

His hand touched one of her more painful bruises, making her wince, making her remember what she had so nearly forgotten. Determinedly she disengaged herself and pulled away. "Please, Sam. Not tonight."

His voice was touched with sudden anger. "Why not tonight? You . . . ?"

"I know, Sam. But I haven't led you on. I want you as much as you want me. Only tonight I can't. There is a reason. A good reason." She steadily met his eyes. "Trust me, Sam. Please."

The anger disappeared from his face, replaced by a promise. "Tomorrow . . . ?"

"Yes, Sam. Tomorrow." Standing well away from him because she didn't entirely trust herself, she said softly: "I love you Sam. I always will."

She turned then and fled to the door. She opened it and ran outside, looking back only once from halfway down the path.

He looked big and strong and indestructible, standing there silhouetted by the light. But he wasn't indestructible. One bullet. . . .

She went on, trying to force that thought from her terrified mind, trying to hold back tears. If he was killed, she would never forgive herself for refusing him.

Hurrying, sometimes running, she made her way back to the rear entrance of the hotel. She went in and climbed the stairs breathlessly to her room.

The door had been repaired. She slammed and locked it behind her and flung herself face downward on the bed.

She prayed, silently but desperately that when it was over Sam would still be safe.

•••

Sam watched Grace disappear into the darkness. He stood there scowling into the night for several moments, troubled by conflicting emotions and desires within himself. He had thought nothing would ever overshadow his thirst for vengeance, but it had. He was a different man than when he had ridden into Los Finados. Then, he hadn't cared whether he lived or died but only about killing the butchers of his brother and teamsters before he was killed himself.

Now it was different. Life held a promise it had never held for him before. He didn't want to die. He wanted to live because there was so much to live for now.

He turned back into the room and blew out the lamps. He went out, pulling the door closed behind him. Warily he stepped down the path to the street and headed for the business section of the town.

Restlessness plagued him. He guessed that it was still not 10:00. Perhaps the restaurant would still be open. If it was not, perhaps he could get something to eat either at the hotel or at one of the saloons.

But wherever he went, he could stir things up. He could begin pushing at Bosma and his friends. He could force them to act whether they were ready to act or not.

Passing the hotel, he glanced up toward Grace's

room, but saw no light. He remembered the bruise on her forehead again, the abrasion on her chin. He wondered if she had really fallen, as she said, and for an instant considered going in and asking the clerk about it. Then he put the thought aside. Now was no time for distrust. If she said she had fallen, then it was the truth. Or if it wasn't, she had a good reason for telling him it was.

Few lights were burning in the hotel, but a couple of lamps shone dimly in the lobby. Down-street, light glowed from two or three saloons. And there was light in the restaurant.

Suddenly hungry, Sam hurried his steps. He found the door locked and knocked on it. He saw Vera Koenig come from the back to open it.

She said in a flat, unfriendly voice: "I've closed for the day."

"Isn't there something you can fix for me? I didn't eat tonight. Besides, I want to talk to you."

She turned that over in her mind a moment, then said reluctantly: "All right. Come on in. The stove's still hot so I suppose I can fix something for you."

"Thanks." He went in, closing the door behind him, and sat down patiently on one of the stools to wait. He heard her moving around in the kitchen, sounding impatient and out of sorts. He could hear steak sizzling and with its smell mingled the aroma of frying potatoes. After a long time, while his hunger mounted, she brought him a plate and filled a coffee cup.

"What did you want to talk about?"

He finished chewing his first bite of steak and said—"Fetters."—before taking the next.

"What about Mister Fetters?"

He glanced at her. She was pretty and she was a nice girl, so far at least. She wanted what all girls want, a husband, a home, and she hadn't found them here. She was afraid she never would, and so was settling for second best.

He said: "You're betting on the wrong horse, Vera. Fetters won't live long enough to give you the things you want."

Her face lost a bit of its color and fright touched her eyes. "Why not? He's perfectly healthy and he's not too old. . . ."

Sam stared straight at her, his eyes like ice. What better way to start the ball rolling than to tell Vera he meant to kill Fetters before he left? It might serve a double purpose, that of dissuading her from what she meant to do and it might scare Fetters enough to panic him. Sam was certain Vera would run straight to Fetters with the news.

He said: "Because I'm going to kill him. It's what I came here for."

Now all the color drained abruptly from her face. Her lips seemed gray. She took an involuntary backward step. Her voice was a terrified whisper. "Why? What has he done?"

Sam glanced at her pityingly, still eating in a way he hoped she would think was callous and unfeeling. "You mean you don't know? How long have you been living here?"

"Almost two years. Don't I know what?"

Sam said contemptuously: "Fetters is a murderer. Oh, not directly. He hasn't got the guts for that. But he's a receiver of stolen goods . . . goods taken from freight wagons after the teamsters have been murdered. He sells them. He shares in the profits from them."

"I can't believe it! Not Mister Fetters!"

Sam took a drink of steaming coffee from the cup. "Ask him, girl. Ask him how it is that he's able to sell articles for less than they cost back East."

He could see that she was beginning to believe, and that she was deeply shocked. He wondered if it was possible that others in the town did not know what Vera so obviously did not.

"You'd murder him in cold blood for money?"

He stared at her with deliberate coldness. "Have you any idea how many men's lives are represented by the goods in Fetters's store? I'm hired to do a job and I'll do it before I leave this town. Killing Fetters is part of that job. How much for the steak?"

Her expression showed shocked unbelief that

he could mention food and the taking of a man's life in the same breath. She said almost inaudibly: "Twenty-five cents."

He tossed a quarter on the counter. Idly he selected a toothpick and stuck it in his mouth.

He got up and walked casually to the door. Turning, he said: "Thanks for opening up for me, Miss Koenig. I was hungry."

Anger heightened the color in her face. Her eyes sparkled with it. "You . . . ! You . . . ! I wish I hadn't fed you! I hope you starve, and you will before I'll serve you again!"

He said: "I'll have this job finished before I get hungry again."

"You mean tonight?"

"Or first thing in the morning." He went out and pulled the door closed behind him. He crossed the street, found a spot in a darkened doorway, and idly watched the restaurant.

He saw Vera run toward the rear of the place. A moment later he saw her blow out the lamps and, almost immediately, come out the door with a shawl around her shoulders. She didn't even take time to lock the door but instead walked swiftly toward the upper end of town where Fetters lived.

Sam felt cruel for having frightened her so but he knew he had done her a favor by telling her the truth. Any decision she made now would be made with her eyes open, knowing exactly what it might cost.

Hidden by darkness in the doorway, Sam waited, watching the street that, at this hour, was almost deserted. A lamp burned dimly in the sheriff's office. A drunk staggered from one of the saloons, fell, got up, and came weaving upstreet past where Sam stood, alternately singing in an off-key, drunken voice and talking to himself.

He waited for fifteen minutes, lounging there comfortably, thinking of Grace, and of Bosma and Hamaker, thinking of the dead Dell and wondering if they had found him yet.

They must have missed him. If either Bosma or Rufus had been past Sam's house, they would have known immediately that something was wrong, for the house was dark. He should have left at least one lamp burning, he thought. It might have delayed the search.

He was about to leave when he saw a dark and monstrously misshapen figure approaching from the upper end of the street. For an instant his flesh crawled. Then he realized who it was. Rufus. Carrying Dell's body flung over his shoulder. The burden and the darkness had combined to give an impression of great size and abnormal shape.

Rufus walked easily, as though he carried no burden at all. He passed Sam on the other side of the street and went on to the sheriff's office. The door, opening, briefly silhouetted him in its square of light. Then it closed behind him.

Sam grinned faintly. They would know who had killed Dell but they'd play hell proving it. They might try, however, with perjured witnesses and false testimony. But not tonight. And by morning Sam hoped the alliance would be beginning to come apart.

He had just as well go home, he thought, and get some sleep. As edgy as Bosma was bound to be right now, caution and good sense might not rule his actions if he caught sight of Sam.

Still grinning slightly, Sam left the doorway and headed along the street toward home.

XIV

Vera Koenig stood frozen for the briefest of moments after the door closed behind Sam Duke. She was in a state of shock, of horror at the callous way he had promised to kill Dixon Fetters before he left the town. He had made monstrous accusations that her mind could not accept. And yet, some uneasiness in the back of her mind told her they were true.

Being true, they would explain so many other things. The meetings down at the sheriff's office that included only Fetters, Pettigrew, Bosma, and Hamaker. The brutal beatings that the sheriff and his deputies sometimes administered to residents of the town.

Hamaker must be the one who ambushed the wagons, she guessed—the one who, with his teamsters, butchered the men driving them. Because Hamaker was always coming into town with a load of goods he hadn't had time to go back East for—goods that eventually ended up in Fetters's store.

Her troubled mind raced. Bosma kept the town in line, having everyone who dared protest beaten. Pettigrew probably was the brains behind the operation, for all his dried-up, mild manner.

She shuddered involuntarily. The dreams she had allowed herself since Fetters had made his veiled proposition began to fade and disappear.

Maybe there still was time—to tell Dixon that Sam Duke intended killing him. Maybe there still was time for them to get away.

Resolutely she hurried around, blowing out the lamps, closing the damper on the stove. Then she hurried to the door and went outside.

She turned uptown toward Dixon Fetters's house. Something within her shrank from the thought of encountering his wife, but this was no time for squeamishness. She hurried on, almost running now.

A single lamp burned in the house, in the parlor at the front. She went up on the porch and twisted the bell in the exact center of the stained glass door.

The door opened almost immediately. Vera's breath sighed out with relief. It was Fetters standing there and not his wife.

Breathlessly she said: "I've got to talk to you."

"Can't it . . . ?" He glanced around nervously toward the stairs. His eyes and face showed what he had been doing up so late. Worrying, and fighting fear.

Vera said firmly: "It can't wait. Not if you want to be alive in the morning, it can't."

Fetters said hoarsely: "All right, come in. Keep your voice down, though. I don't want my wife. . . ."

Vera went in and Fetters closed the door. He led her along the hall to the parlor.

He looked tired and his fight against his fear had obviously been unsuccessful. "What's this all about?"

"Sam Duke. That stranger in town. He was in a few minutes ago and said he was going to kill you. He said that was why he came here and that he'd do it before he left."

Fetters's hands were shaking violently. "Why should he . . . ?" He fished for a cigar, got it out, but couldn't seem to light it. He sat there chewing on it and staring with blank and hopeless eyes at the wall.

Vera felt something sink within her. It was true, then. Fetters's expression, his manner, his obvious terror confirmed it. But his evident helplessness brought out something in Vera's heart she had not previously realized was there. Pity. Something that might have been love. A kind of strange fulfillment because now there was someone who needed her.

She said softly: "There's only one thing you can do. Get away. Now. Tonight. Before it's too late."

"I can't. . . ." He looked around the room. "My wife . . . this house . . . the store. I can't, that's all. Bosma will handle Duke."

"Don't be too sure of that. Have you looked at him? Have you talked to him? There's something terrible about him that frightens me. I have the feeling he can handle a dozen Bosmas and still come out on top. When he said he was going to kill you . . . I can't explain it, but I knew he would do exactly what he said he would no matter who stood in the way."

"But all this . . . I've spent my life. . . ."

"And you'll lose it if you don't listen to me. Have you any money?"

"Not much of my own. Maybe a thousand."

"What do you mean, of your own? Do you have some that belongs to someone else?"

Something was growing in his eyes, plainly the birth of a new idea. He said: "The money in the safe . . . you know I bank for the town. Some of yours is there."

"How much is there in all?" Vera's voice was suddenly breathless. Maybe it was possible, after all. Money could do anything. It could buy protection. It could take them far from Los Finados, far enough for them to be safe and free.

He shrugged. "I don't know offhand. Maybe ten or fifteen thousand."

Vera's breath sighed out. "Do you want to live, Dixon? Do you want me?"

"You know damned well I do."

Something made Vera look around and she saw Fetters's wife standing in the doorway.

The woman's graying hair was undone and lay in braids down either side of her shriveled breasts. She was clad in a long nightgown and looked every year of her age. But something in her eyes—fury greater than Vera had ever seen before. Outrage. She screeched: "You harlot! You slut! Get out of my house!"

Vera knew she stood at a fork in the road but she didn't hesitate about which path she would take. Along one road lay more of what she'd had so far—a grubby restaurant in which she fed dirty men—forlorn hope that a man would come along who she could love and who would love her in return and want to marry her.

Along the other road was getting away from Los Finados—Dixon Fetters, who she had convinced herself she loved—money and all the things money could buy. She said thinly: "No. Not until Dixon is ready to come with me."

"Am I hearing right? He won't go with you! He's my husband! Dixon, send this trollop away! Get her out of here!"

Vera looked at Dixon Fetters. She knew, as she looked, what kind of man she was getting. One who would never quite stand and face the world on his own two feet. One who would let her face it for him, and stand between the world and him. Not exactly what she'd had in mind for a husband, but she had made her choice. She said: "Don't talk to him. Talk to me."

"I'll talk to you! I'll . . . !" Screaming the words, Mrs. Fetters came rushing across the room.

But Vera was ready for her, younger and

stronger, too. She caught Mrs. Fetters's wrists in her hands.

Mrs. Fetters screamed, and cried, and fought. She kicked Vera in the shins with her bare feet. She tried to bite.

Fetters leaped to his feet. He roared: "Stop it! Stop it, for Christ's sake!" He crossed the room, seized his wife by the arm, and wrenched her away from Vera. He shouted: "I'm leaving you! With her! Damn you, you've nagged and screeched at me for the last time! Shut up, I tell you! Shut up!"

For an instant her eyes were stunned. Then they were filled with fury again, greater if possible than before. She began to scream epithets at him. She fought free of his grasp and slapped him resoundingly on the cheek.

Something ugly showed briefly in Fetters's eyes, something not at all in keeping with his character. Vera was sure he had never struck his wife, but he did so now, with an enormous, closed fist, the way he would strike a man.

Vera knew that in that blow was the sudden release of all the enforced self-discipline of years. In it was suppressed hatred, and retaliation for all the humiliation he had taken from her. If he had possessed a weapon, he might have killed her then. But his only weapon was his fist.

The blow struck her in the middle of the forehead with a sound like that of a cleaver biting through meat and bone on a butcher's block. She was flung backward. She struck the wall, unconscious, slid down it to the floor, and lay there in a crumpled position.

Fetters stared at his unconscious wife dazedly. He muttered: "Damn you! Damn you!"

Vera said soothingly: "Come on, Dixon. There's no time to lose."

He turned and looked at her, his eyes confused. She went to him, raised her face, and kissed him lightly on the mouth. "It's all right now. Come on."

He stared at her as he might have stared at a complete stranger, without comprehension. He turned his head and glanced uneasily at his wife's crumpled body on the floor. He wiped the back of his hand across his mouth where Vera had kissed him. "I've got to see Bosma," he said. "I've got to see him right away."

"No, Dixon. Get what you want to take with you and meet me at the store."

He looked emptily at her, plainly not really seeing her at all. He was in a state of shock, she guessed, brought on by fear and confusion. She said firmly: "Get what you need and meet me at the store. How many horses do you have?"

"Two."

"Where are they, in the stable behind the house?"

"Yes."

"I'll saddle them up. I'll have to go to my place for some things, but I'll meet you at the store in ten or fifteen minutes. All right?"

He nodded numbly. "All right."

Vera watched him doubtfully for several moments. Then with a little shrug, she turned and went out the door.

Fetters stood utterly still for several minutes after Vera left. He stared across the room at the crumpled body of his wife. She wasn't dead. He could see her body move regularly with her breathing. As though dazed, he turned and walked out of the house without even bothering to put on a hat.

He was big and could lift a hundred and fifty pounds with scarcely an effort. Physically he was a match for any man in town, even Rufus. But he was not a strong man and never had been. He had allowed his wife to bully and manage him for years. He had no moral strength at all.

Right now he needed Bosma the way a man dying of thirst needs water. At a fast walk, he hurried toward the main street and, having reached it, along it toward the sheriff's office.

Remembering Vera's words, he glanced often to right and left, toward the dark shadows in doorways, toward the black and empty passageways between some of the buildings.

The saloons were still open. He needed a drink tonight more than he had ever needed it in his life before. But he didn't dare. Tonight more than ever before he needed his mind clear.

There was a light in the sheriff's office. He opened the door. Bosma was inside and he swung to glare ferociously at Fetters. "What the hell do you want?"

Fetters glanced toward the couch in the corner and his hands began to twitch. Dell lay there, face up, staring at the ceiling with glazed eyes. There was a hollow in his skull partially filled with torn flesh and blood-soaked hair. Blood and dirt had mingled over one entire side of his face and dried there until it looked like an enormous scab. And Dell was very dead.

He whispered: "How . . . ? Who killed him?"

"That god-damned Duke, that's who. And I'll get him if it's the last thing I ever do." He fixed Fetters with a cold and angry stare. "I asked what you wanted."

"I want you to get rid of Duke. He threatened me tonight. He told Vera he was going to kill me before he left town. He said either tonight or early tomorrow."

"I'll get rid of him. You go on home. Get off the street and stay out of my way."

Fetters's voice was scarcely audible. "Why did he kill Dell?"

"I had Dell watching his house. Some of the townsmen were there tonight and I wanted to know who they were. Dell was supposed to tell me, but he can't do it now."

"Why don't you arrest Duke?"

"Arrest him? You damned fool, I can't. I haven't a bit of proof. Not like Pettigrew wants."

Fetters began to tremble even more violently than he had before. Bosma wasn't giving him the reassurance he had come to get. He had expected the sheriff to promise him Duke would be dead before morning. But Pettigrew was running the show and Pettigrew had said Duke wasn't to be killed outright. He had to be tried and hanged so that whoever might show up later looking for him would be unable to prove murder against those who had gotten rid of him.

"How long is it going to take?"

"How the hell should I know?" Bosma snapped irritably. "Maybe a couple of days, maybe a week. Pettigrew wants it done right so there won't be any questions afterward."

"But Duke told Vera he was going to kill me . . . either tonight or tomorrow morning."

Bosma grinned at him evilly. "If he does, we'll hang him for it. That make you feel better?"

Fetters felt as though he were coming apart. He wanted to hit Bosma and knock him down just as he had his wife. He took a step toward the sheriff, stopped when Bosma said softly: "Don't move, Fetters, or I'll blow you in two."

Fetters croaked: "I'm getting out of this damned town. You're supposed to protect the citizens. If you can't. . . ."

Bosma began to chuckle. His face turned red and his chuckle grew into a laugh. He choked: "You stupid fool, do you know how funny that sounds?"

"There's nothing funny about being killed." Outrage was strong in Fetters's voice, an almost childish outrage that recognized its own ridiculousness and increased because it did. He turned and stamped out of the office, slamming the door resoundingly behind.

At least he was through being terrified. And his mind had been made up for him. Vera was right. They should take the money and get out of town. Tonight. While there still was time. She had said she would bring the horses to the store. She should be there right now.

He hurried angrily along the street. Duke wouldn't shoot him from ambush. Duke wasn't that kind. Besides, the man was probably at home in bed right now.

He had until morning, he told himself. And by morning he and Vera could be thirty miles away.

While he was still half a block away, he saw the dim shapes of the horses in front of the store. Drawing nearer, he saw Vera standing on the walk.

He began to think of a life that held no fear and no guilt, but only Vera and the money in the safe. They could go thousands of miles away. With some of the money that was left, he could start another store.

Suddenly he felt safe with the blanket of darkness close around him on all sides. He hurried toward her, fishing for his key.

XV

For several moments after Fetters left, Bosma stared closely at the door, frowning to himself. Damn! Fetters was acting like a scared rabbit. Duke had threatened him and already Fetters was beginning to come apart.

At least, he thought, Duke was coming out into the open now. He had killed Dell to prevent him from telling Bosma the names of the townspeople who had gathered at his house tonight. He had threatened Fetters through Vera.

But why had he done it? Bosma was not long in coming up with an answer. Duke had picked Fetters as the weakest of the four. He was trying to break the man, trying to put an opening wedge into the solidarity of the combine through its weakest link.

Good strategy, thought Bosma. Duke was no fool. But it wasn't going to work. They couldn't afford to let it work. He wondered worriedly—what would Fetters do? Would he go to Duke and blab to save his own neck? He doubted it. He even doubted if it would do Fetters any good. Duke probably already knew everything he needed to know.

Would Fetters cut and run? That was the most likely thing for him to do, decided the sheriff. That would be Fetters's natural approach to a problem he couldn't solve.

He should have reassured the man, he thought. By not reassuring him, he had played right into Sam Duke's hands.

Maybe he'd better keep an eye on Fetters. He went back into the cells at the rear of the building and stirred Rufus who was sleeping on a cot in one of them. The man stirred, grunted protestingly, and then sat up. "What's the matter?"

"I've got to go out for a while. Come on up front and keep an eye on things."

"Something happened?"

"Not yet."

"Going after Duke?"

Bosma stared down at him. He said: "Maybe. Maybe I am at that in a roundabout sort of way." An idea had just come to him, one that made the corners of his mouth lift in a humorless smile. If Fetters was cleaning out his safe—if he was getting ready to run—what better way to frame Sam Duke than for Fetters's death? Vera would testify in court that Sam had threatened him. Duke had even specified the time he would murder Fetters. Tonight or early tomorrow. There wasn't a jury in the world that wouldn't convict him and sentence him to hang. Even an impartial jury would do that. Particularly if part of the money cleaned out of the town's makeshift bank was found on him or in his house.

Bosma's grin widened as he went back through the office and out the front door. There was even profit in the scheme. He could pocket $2,000 or $3,000 of the money and nobody would be the wiser. It would simply be assumed that Fetters had embezzled it before he died.

Maybe things would work out after all, he thought as he pulled the door closed silently behind him. He had never liked the idea of a weakling like Fetters being part of the operation. It had seemed to him when they started that they'd have done better to let Hamaker open another store in competition with Fetters to dispose of the stolen goods. They could have run Fetters out of business in two or three months. And Hamaker could be relied upon.

But with Fetters dead, with Sam Duke executed for his murder, they could go on again, more solidly than before. Hamaker would simply take over the store.

Quietly he walked up the street. He took each step carefully so that he would not make any noise. Vera was probably with Fetters. They were probably planning to run away together.

He could make out the shapes of two horses as he drew near the store. He had been right. Fetters wouldn't try taking two horses just for himself. Vera must be going with him.

If she was with him now, and she probably was, her presence presented problems. He didn't dare let her see him. He might be able to scare her into testifying that Sam Duke had killed Fetters but it would be a whole lot better if she really believed he had.

He'd have to try and slip up behind her without being seen. If he could do that, and knock her out. . . .

The horses eyed him nervously as he came abreast of the store. The door gaped open and it was completely dark inside. He could hear voices, softly conversing far back in the depths of the store.

He tried to remember where the creaking board was just inside the door. Funny. He'd stepped on that creaking board at least a thousand times but now he found it difficult to remember exactly where it was. If he didn't enter normally—if he stepped aside just as he entered—the chances were he'd avoid it.

He stepped into the doorway and immediately moved to the right. He held his breath, waiting for the board to creak, but it did not.

It was darker here than it had been outside and he waited, breathing softly, until his eyes began to accustom themselves. Fetters helped him by striking a match back there where he kept the safe. By its light, Bosma moved as swiftly as a cat. He covered half the distance between himself and the pair before it burned down and was dropped with a muttered curse.

Bosma halted as soon as it went out. There was plenty of time, he thought. To hurry now would be to jeopardize the whole plan. If he knocked something off a counter—if Fetters and the girl were warned—he'd have to kill them both and he didn't want to do that. He wanted Vera alive to testify.

Their voices droned on and after several moments another match was struck, this time by Vera. She held it aloft while Fetters opened the safe and swung back the door.

It *squeaked* thunderously as he did. Bosma took advantage of the noise to move closer. When he stopped, he was less than fifteen feet away.

He breathed shallowly, softly as Fetters reached back into the safe and withdrew the money box. He smiled slightly but without humor. His guess had been right. Fetters was taking all the money belonging to the town, dumping the box into a canvas sack.

Vera struck another match. As it flared, Bosma rushed, gun in hand.

He struck Vera on the side of the head from behind and she crumpled forward without a sound. The match she was holding fell from her fingers and flickered out.

Bosma cursed softly under his breath. Like a damned fool, he'd been watching the flame of that match. Now, with it gone, he was temporarily blind.

Fetters didn't wait to see what had happened to Vera or to engage her assailant. He lumbered to his feet and fled heavily toward the door.

A stack of buckets *clattered* in the aisle as he blundered into them. The racket was thunderous. Bosma raced in his wake, cursing savagely. The damned fool would wake the town.

Suddenly now, with his plan in jeopardy, he wondered what Pettigrew would have to say. Pettigrew had told him to clear whatever plan he used with him.

He caught a glimpse of Fetters silhouetted against the lighter square of light that marked the door. He raised his gun and fired instantly without sighting, by feel alone.

Fetters stumbled and sprawled face downward just inside the door of the store. The canvas sack *thumped* on the floor.

Bosma hauled up, panting, beside his body. He pointed the gun down at Fetters's upper body and fired twice more. Then he seized the canvas sack and stepped outside.

Keeping close to the building wall, he edged along until he came to a passageway leading back toward the alley. He ducked into it and ran. When he reached the alley, he stuck his hand into the canvas sack, opened the money box, got a handful of currency, and withdrew it. He dropped the heavy sack into the narrow space between a board fence and a shed.

The currency went into his pocket. Running, he went along the alley to the next street, along that to the main street again, and along that toward the store where a startled and sleepy-eyed group of townspeople were already beginning to congregate.

His voice was filled with authority for all that he was out of breath. "What the hell's going on? I heard gunshots."

An unidentified voice said: "It's Fetters, Sheriff. He's been robbed and killed."

"Anybody got a lantern?"

"Fetters keeps one just inside the store. I'll see if I can find it."

Bosma waited while his breathing became normal again. He heard the townsman fumbling just inside the door for the lantern. After several moments a match flared and shortly the lantern began to glow, its light growing stronger momentarily. Bosma stepped into the store and knelt beside Fetters's body just inside the door.

He put his head down on Fetters's chest and listened for heartbeat or breathing. There was nothing. Fetters was dead.

"Anybody see anything?" He waited tensely for a reply. It was probable that they had not. People awakened by sudden sharp sounds usually did not get to a place from which they could see anything for several minutes.

Nobody answered. He took the lantern and walked back into the store. Vera was stirring. He put the lantern down and helped her to a sitting position. "What happened? Did you see any-thing?"

"Dixon . . . Mister Fetters . . . is he all right?"

"He's dead, Vera. Did you see who did it?"

She shook her head, numbness and shock in her eyes. Then, as comprehension began to seep into her mind, she said: "It was that stranger, Sam Duke."

"Did you see him?"

"No, but he threatened to kill Mister Fetters. He said he was going to do it tonight or early tomorrow morning."

"When did he say that, Vera?" Bosma glanced up at the faces of the townsmen who had followed him into the store.

"Tonight . . . in the restaurant." Bosma could see her mind beginning to work. She went on: "I went up to his house to warn him. Missus Fetters misunderstood. She thought there was some-thing . . . that Mister Fetters and I. . . ." She stopped helplessly, then went on determinedly: "He was worried about the money in the safe. He thought Duke must be after that. So we came down here to get it out and put it where it would be safe."

Bosma could scarcely repress a smile. Vera had covered herself well. Now if Mrs. Fetters didn't say any of the wrong things. . . . But even if she did, it wouldn't matter much. Vera was covering for herself, getting involved already in half truths and outright lies. The deeper she became involved, the more determined she would be that Sam Duke was the one who had spoiled everything.

So far, things had worked out perfectly. He got to his feet and asked: "Will a couple of you take her home? Then get Grace Marr. She'll know what to do."

Two of the townsmen helped Vera to her feet and walked out of the store with her.

Bosma said: "I want a posse to get Sam Duke."

"Figure he ran, Sheriff?"

Bosma grinned sourly. "I doubt it. He'd know we'd catch him if he did. He probably went back home. I'll lay you ten to one we'll find him in bed, acting innocent as hell."

"Let's go get him, then! I had two hundred dollars in that safe!"

There was a chorus of angry exclamations from the others. Bosma picked up the lantern, his face grim and unsmiling now. Even Pettigrew couldn't have done better than this, he thought. Sam Duke's goose was cooked.

XVI

Grace Marr's window overlooked the street. It was a kind of bay window, projecting out, with a center pane of glass and two narrower panes, one at each side of it. By putting her head close to the center glass, she could see both ways along the street. Both side panes were on hinges and could be opened, thus allowing air to flow into the room from either direction.

For a long time after entering the room, she lay face downward on the bed, trembling both with fear for Sam and fear that Bosma would return and finish what he had started earlier.

She wished she had a gun with which to defend herself. She had never used one, but if Bosma came back, she knew she could use it against him.

The town quieted and the streets emptied of the few late walkers. A piano still *tinkled* softly from one of the saloons downstreet and occasionally a dog would bark, but otherwise there was no sound.

Gradually Grace calmed. Nothing was going to happen tonight. But she wouldn't sleep just the same. She couldn't.

She got up and nervously paced the room, still without lighting a lamp. The piano stopped *tinkling* and even the dogs seemed to have gone to sleep.

The sounds of horses' hoofs in the street drew her to the window. She saw them coming, two of them, being led by someone she couldn't recognize because of the darkness. Someone small, like a woman or a boy. They stopped in front of Fetters's store.

Several moments later she heard hurrying footsteps on the boardwalk and shortly thereafter saw a larger figure join the first.

Fetters was unmistakable because of his size. The other must be a woman, perhaps Fetters's wife.

She wondered what they were doing. Why were they here, with horses, at this hour of the night?

There could only be one answer to that. They were leaving town, running away, and had probably come here to get the money out of the safe inside the store.

Grace didn't move, having no desire to interfere. Fetters was one of the ring, but to have him gone would satisfy Grace's hatred of him as effectively as his death would have done. Let him go, she thought. His absence would mean one less that Sam would have to face, one less that he would have to fight.

She continued to watch, shivering slightly in the cool air blowing into the room. The pair tied the horses and went into the store. For a while, then, all was quiet.

A strange feeling of uneasiness began to trouble

her, but until she heard other steps coming along the boardwalk from the direction of the sheriff's office she failed to understand its cause. Looking down, she saw a third shadow pass beneath her window, this one as unmistakable as the figure of Fetters had been. This one was the sheriff.

He moved stealthily, and would have been unheard by Grace except for the fact that she was almost directly above him. He entered the store as stealthily as he had come along the walk.

The normal precautions of a law officer, perhaps, entering premises where he suspected a crime was in progress. But Grace was not convinced.

Something told her it was not as simple as it appeared. Something told her Sam Duke ought to be warned at once, while there still was time. There was threat to him in this.

Yet she stood frozen, watching. The first gunshot came as no surprise, nor did the second and the third, louder and apparently closer to the door.

No shouts. No order to halt. Just those gunshots, racketing without warning through the night.

The compulsion to run and warn Sam was stronger now, yet she did not move. She had to be sure. She had to know.

Bosma emerged stealthily from the door of Fetters's store. The horses fidgeted briefly, startled by the gunshots and by his appearance.

They quieted when the sounds were not repeated, when Bosma disappeared into a dark passage-way between two buildings.

Lights began to go on, above store buildings where the storekeepers had living quarters. In some of the rooms of the hotel. Dark figures began to move along the street toward Fetters's store.

They clustered before it and Grace heard a sleepy, querulous voice: "Where the hell's the sheriff?"

Running steps on the boardwalk beneath her window. And for a second time Bosma passed, with no stealthiness at all this time.

Grace waited no longer. It was plain to her now what had happened in the store. Bosma had surprised Fetters and his companion emptying the safe. He had entered and murdered them without even calling a challenge. He had then slipped out, gone between two buildings to the alley, and from there returned to the street in time to arrive as though just coming from his office down the street.

Her uneasiness was plain to her now. Fetters was dead, killed by Bosma, who had caught him robbing his own safe. But Sam was the one they were going to blame for this. He wouldn't have a chance. Pettigrew and Bosma would see to that.

She ran to her closet and snatched her nightgown from its hook. Stuffing it under her arm, she seized a key ring from the dresser top, flung open the door, and fled along the hall toward the rear stairs that led down to the alley behind the hotel.

All she could think was that she had to help Sam. And the only way she knew to help him was to prove he could not have been at the store when Fetters was shot.

She reached the alley unseen and fled along it toward the upper end of town. At the first cross street she stopped, peering breathlessly to right and left. Other townspeople would have been aroused by the commotion at the store and would be streaming along the street toward it. And if she were seen, her chance of helping Sam would disappear.

She saw two shadowy figures pass at the intersection, so instead of hurrying up the cross street, she crossed it instead and entered the alley beyond. She went another full block before she turned toward the house she had rented Sam.

Her time was getting short. The townspeople would be aroused and infuriated at the thought of losing the savings they had deposited with Fetters at the store. Bosma would be anxious to lead them to Sam.

Her lungs seemed to be on fire but she didn't slow her pace. She fell once as she turned into Sam's street, but got up and went on, limping slightly. Nearing the house, she selected a key from the ring by feel.

Behind her, she could hear the low murmur of angry voices as they came along the street, little more than a block behind. She hurried up on the porch, inserted her key, and opened the door as silently as she could.

She closed it without locking it and went immediately to the bedroom, saying softly and breathlessly as she entered: "Sam, stay where you are. It's Grace."

He grunted softly with startled surprise. The gun, which he had snatched when he first heard the door, made a heavy noise as he laid it on the floor beside the bed.

In darkness, her face flaming, Grace removed her clothes. She slipped the nightgown over her head, then picked up the clothes, and flung them into the closet. She got into bed with Sam as the first heavy steps sounded on the porch.

Sam tensed and reached for the gun again, but Grace put her arms around his neck, holding him, whispering softly: "Sam, stay where you are. Muss my hair a little and don't touch the gun or get up when they knock. Make them come in. They've got to find us together here."

"Why . . . ?"

"Sam, don't question me. There isn't time."

He murmured softly, almost sleepily: "Damn."

"What's the matter?"

"I've wanted you in my arms ever since I met you. And now that you're here, there are people all over the place."

"Sam, they're coming. . . ." She heard the outer door bang open, heard their heavy steps in the house itself. For an instant terror touched her heart. What if she had miscalculated? What if Bosma killed Sam while he lay here help-lessly?

The bedroom door slammed open. Lantern light and angry men crowded into the room.

Sam sat up, growling an angry, outraged: "What the god-damned hell . . . ? Get out of here!"

The expression on Bosma's face was almost ludicrous. It was filled with shock, with unbelief, with frustrated and growing fury. Yet Grace knew he was helpless. He had brought a dozen townsmen to witness Sam's arrest and now those very witnesses prevented what he might other-wise have done. Not a one of those with him would believe Sam had killed Fetters or that he had been out of his bed tonight.

Bosma croaked weakly: "Where were you half an hour ago, Duke?"

"You dumb bastard!" Sam roared. "Where the hell do you think I was? Where does it look like I was? Get out of here before I blow your god-damned head off!"

Bosma's eyes were murderous, and became even more so when a man back in the parlor chuckled: "I know where I'd 'a' been, was I him. Right where he was, by God."

Grace's face was scarlet and hot with shame. This was so sordid—at least in appearance it was. But she didn't care. She knew she would do exactly the same thing again. She had won. She had saved Sam's life. What did it matter if she had ruined her own reputation in the process? What did it matter if every man she met on the street of this town would henceforth look her insolently up and down and snicker as she passed?

They backed out of the room, carrying their lantern, and Bosma, balked and furious, backed out with them. Grace heard them whispering among themselves as they went out the front door. She heard a loud, suggestive laugh.

Her whole body felt hot. She began to tremble and tears streamed down her cheeks.

Sam held her gently. "Tell me now. What happened?"

"Bosma caught Mister Fetters robbing his own safe. He slipped in and killed him, I think. At least I heard three shots. Then he came out and ducked between two buildings and disappeared. A few minutes later he came up the street and went into the front door again. It was so sly . . . I thought he must be planning to say you'd done it so I did the only thing I could think of. There wasn't time for anything else."

"I'd say you did exactly right. You saved my

neck. Bosma would have found part of the money here in the house when he got to searching it. And I'd have been hanged for sure."

She stirred and tried to pull away. "I've got to go now, Sam."

"Your reputation is ruined. You know that, don't you?"

"It doesn't matter. I won't be here very long."

"I'll make an honest woman out of you before we leave." There was a teasing quality in his voice so gentle it made her smile faintly in the darkness. "And you don't have to go right away. Staying won't hurt your reputation any more than it's already hurt."

"Sam? Are you suggesting . . . ?"

He kissed her, long and hard, leaving her breathless and without the desire to protest. Her arms crept up around his neck. Her body was soft and yielding against his own hard, insistent one. Male and driving, yet with great gentleness, too, he made her forget the town, the place, the reasons both of them were here. For these few indescribably wonderful moments there was nothing but the two of them, needing and wanting and taking, yet giving, too.

When it was over, she lay spent in the crook of his hard, muscular arm and whispered: "Sam, we still can leave. We could get up and dress and pack. We could be gone before the sun came up."

His arm tightened. His cheek, rough as

sandpaper, touched her own. "Do you think they'd let us now? We wouldn't get fifty miles."

"No, I don't suppose we would."

"I can finish it up tomorrow, I think. They're doing what I hoped they would . . . getting scared and fighting among themselves. Bosma has all the money now and don't think for a minute the others will take it lying down."

"You don't think they'll all kill each other off?"

"Not altogether, maybe. But part of it will be done for me, and I can finish up the rest. I'd never be able to forget if I ran out now. And neither would you, for all you think you would right now."

She tried to hold her body still, to keep it from trembling. She had to get up and leave now, before the sky turned light. She didn't dare risk letting Sam see any of the marks Bosma had left on her.

But she could stay a little while. There were hours left before the dawn turned the sky to gray. She could stay, and, if she never had anything else, she would have had Sam for tonight. All to herself. In safety and, for these short hours, without fear.

XVII

Bosma was furious as he stalked out of Sam's house, and the chuckles and ribald comments of the townsmen he had brought with him did not reduce his rage. Damn Pettigrew for insisting that Duke be eliminated legally!

At the street, he stopped. Without looking at any of the men with him directly, he said sourly: "Go on home. If I need you again, I'll let you know."

Something in the tone of his voice stopped their talk, forestalled any protest.

Bosma growled: "Whoever robbed that safe and killed Fetters . . . I'll get him, don't worry about that. I'll get every damn' cent of the money back, too."

They dispersed, heading for their separate homes. Bosma stood and stared at Sam Duke's house several long moments before he turned away.

There was a strange feeling of impending disaster in him—one he had never experienced before. It was as though he watched the starting of an avalanche high on a mountain hillside— watched it start with a single rock that bounded down toward him gathering others as it came. He seemed powerless to move and get out of its way, powerless to stop it now that it had started.

Sam Duke was that single rock that had started

the avalanche. The others he gathered as he came were the people of the town, sickened and angered by the merciless brutality of those who ruled it. Now they would be further angered by the loss of their money that had been kept in Fetters's safe. Unless he pretended to find it and gave it back.

Fetters and Dell had already been overwhelmed. Who, Bosma wondered uneasily, was going to be next? It wouldn't be him. He was going to see to that. Head down, scowling, he scuffed along toward his office at the lower end of town. Maybe he'd be smart to take the money that had been in Fetters's safe and get out of town. Maybe he was a fool to stay. And yet, the thought of one man successfully defeating the whole rich scheme developed by the four of them made him rage helplessly. To hell with Pettigrew and his notion that others would follow Duke. If they did, they could be handled when they came. The thing to do with Sam Duke was kill him, right away, in any way possible. Once he was dead, the town would grow tame again quickly enough.

Yet the feeling of impending disaster stayed with him. He paused at Fetters's store and closed the door, locking it with the key that was still in the lock. He dropped the key into his pocket and stood before the door, staring watchfully up and down the street.

Nothing stirred along its entire length. The town

slept, and the darkness was a blanket over it. The air was beginning to chill with the coming of dawn. Even the dogs were still.

Satisfied that he was not observed, Bosma left the store and entered the same passageway he had entered immediately following the killing of Fetters. At its end he paused, then vaulted the fence, and reached for the money sack.

He found it at once, re-vaulted the fence, and returned to the street. It was still deserted.

The sack was heavy and hard to conceal. He put it under his coat, holding it there with his left hand. He continued down the street until he reached his office.

He peered inside. Rufus was sleeping in the chair, his head back, his mouth open. Bosma entered silently. He went immediately into the cells at the rear, taking care to make no noise.

There was a covered bucket in each cell for the use of the prisoners. All were clean and it was doubtful if anyone would ever look into them as long as the cells were unoccupied. Carefully Bosma lifted the lid of one and placed the money bag inside. He replaced the lid silently.

He returned to the front office and stood looking at Rufus with distaste. He would have to make up his mind right now. Tomorrow might be too late. And once it was made up, he'd have to continue along the course he had chosen to the end.

He scowled. Slow anger began to grow in him,

compounded of injured pride that one man could so upset a perfect scheme, greed for more of the money that had come so easily, and reluctance to give up his position as undisputed ruler of the town.

His jaw set into an angry line as he made his decision within himself. To hell with Sam Duke! He was only a man and he could be killed. To hell with Pettigrew! Whatever he did, he was not going to quit and run.

While Pettigrew was not in evidence at the store immediately after Fetters was killed, he was watching from a doorway farther up the street—uneasily and with a concerned expression on his face.

He was under no illusions as to what had happened. He knew Fetters and knew Bosma, too. Fetters had been robbing his own safe, intending to take the money and run off with Vera Koenig. Bosma caught him at it and killed him.

Pettigrew didn't really care about Fetters's death. Fetters was not an indispensable link in the chain. But he did care that Bosma now had all the money, including $6,000 or $7,000 belonging to Pettigrew himself. And so, unseen by anyone, he continued to watch the developments within the town from the darkness just outside the ring of light cast by the lanterns the townsmen had lighted.

He followed Bosma and his hastily gathered

posse to Sam Duke's house, approving Bosma's plan and hoping it would work. He saw Bosma come out again, without Sam, and from the comments and laughter of the townsmen understood what had happened.

Duke was no fool, and neither was Grace Marr. And now the chance to convict and execute Sam Duke was gone.

The same feeling of impending disaster that troubled Bosma began to trouble Pettigrew. Everything seemed to be going wrong.

His sense of uneasiness increased. In possession of the money from Fetters's safe, Bosma might choose to flee, leaving Pettigrew and Hamaker to handle Duke. And Hamaker couldn't handle either Duke or the town the way Bosma could. He shivered slightly, and not from cold.

Watching, he saw the crowd disperse. He followed Bosma, saw him lock Fetters's store, then disappear into the passageway. He saw him reappear and walk downstreet toward the jail.

Pettigrew halted in a dark doorway, frowning to himself. A couple of courses were open to him now. He could go down to Bosma's office and demand a split, or he could wake Hamaker and the two of them could force a division.

The first way was dangerous. Bosma had killed once tonight and wouldn't hesitate to kill again. Yet the second alternative meant the money would be split three ways instead of two.

Greed and fear fought a brief battle within his mind and fear won. He turned and headed for Hamaker's shack a block beyond the freight warehouse a short distance from the hotel.

He had to pound insistently for several minutes before the door opened. He knew Hamaker was standing there, a gun in his hand, even though he couldn't see the man. He said breathlessly: "It's Pettigrew. I've got to talk to you."

Hamaker growled a stream of profanity, but he ended it with: "All right. Come on in. But get it over with quick."

He went in and waited uneasily while Hamaker lighted a lamp. The room smelled of stale bedding. He glanced once at the burly teamster in his dirty long underwear, then glanced away. He said: "Some things have happened. I suppose you slept right through them."

"Maybe. What things?"

"Fetters got scared. He cleaned out his own safe and was getting ready to run. Bosma caught him and killed him."

Hamaker shrugged disinterestedly. "So I peddle the stuff we steal. We don't need Fetters anyhow."

Pettigrew snapped irritably: "I'm not thinking of Fetters. I'm thinking about all that money. Bosma's got it now."

"So let him have it. He hasn't got any of mine."

"But he's got mine. And he's got the town's. If

they don't get it back first thing in the morning, they're going to be hard to handle."

"We can handle 'em."

Pettigrew said snappishly: "Damn you, I want you to go down to Bosma's office with me and demand that he split that money with us."

"I thought you said it had to be given back to the townspeople."

"Well, part of it does. Unless we want to quit and get the hell out of here."

Hamaker stared at him contemptuously. "Do your own damn' dirty work, Pettigrew. I've got my money in a safe place. Work it out with Bosma yourself and let me go back to sleep."

Pettigrew said angrily: "I'm not asking you to go with me. I'm telling you!"

Hamaker stared at him with icy, contemptuous eyes. "You don't tell me anything, little man. Now get out of here before I take you apart."

Pettigrew thought of the Derringer he had concealed in the pocket of his vest. Right now he wanted to kill Hamaker.

He fought himself for control. Hamaker got up and came toward him. Pettigrew's courage evaporated. He scuttled for the door. He heard it slam behind him and saw the lamp go out.

He stood trembling with rage on the sagging porch, then stalked down the weed-grown path to the street.

He began to think as Fetters had—of getting out

of town—of taking all the money he could lay his hands on and running, fast and far. Only Bosma stood in the way.

He fingered the Derringer as he walked. He'd give Bosma a chance to split the money first. But if Bosma wouldn't split. . . .

Hurriedly and determinedly, smarting under the humiliation of running from Hamaker, of having his authority flaunted, he went toward the jail, in which a lamp still burned.

He stopped immediately outside and peered in. He saw Rufus asleep in the chair, his mouth open, snoring. He saw Bosma inspecting the guns in the rack. Dell's body lay on the office couch.

Pettigrew was briefly appalled at the amount of damage Sam Duke had already done here in Los Finados. If he wasn't stopped soon. . . . Perhaps he had been wrong in insisting that Duke be hanged for some trumped-up crime. Maybe he should have let Bosma kill him outright. To hell with the way it looked.

He opened the door and went inside. Bosma turned to glance at him.

There was something of defiance in Bosma's glance. "I tried it your way and it didn't work."

Pettigrew said: "I know."

"How the hell was I supposed to know Grace Marr would . . . ?"

"You couldn't know, I guess." Pettigrew kept looking at Bosma, obscurely pleased at what he saw in Bosma's eyes. Physically Bosma wasn't afraid of him, but then their relations had been on an intellectual level rather than on a physical one. Intellectually Bosma did fear him and this was in sharp contrast to his experience with Hamaker who, he told himself, was a pig too stupid to fear anything.

He asked accusingly: "What happened to the money that was in Fetters's safe?"

Now Bosma's eyes shifted and he knew the man was going to lie to him. Bosma said: "I don't know. Damned if I do. It just disappeared. Someone in the crowd must have picked it up in the confusion. I'll find out who tomorrow. He'll be sorry, whoever he is."

Pettigrew said flatly: "You're a liar, Karl. Not only a liar, you're a greedy, stupid one."

Bosma's face flushed and his glance swung angrily to meet Pettigrew's. Now there was something new in the sheriff's eyes, something that made Pettigrew's chest feel tight and cold.

He turned partially and casually stuck his hand into the vest pocket where the Derringer was. One shot, he thought. The gun held but one shot and was effective only at short range. Without looking directly at Bosma, he said: "I want half of it, Karl. And I want to go when you do." He tried to make his voice sound contemptuous, superior, and sure, but it didn't come out that way. It came out shaky and scared. He waited while the silence between them grew until it was almost thunderous.

Then Bosma began to laugh, softly at first but with growing hilarity. "And I thought . . . ," he choked. "You're a fool, Pettigrew, but I'm a bigger one. For ever listening to you at all. For ever thinking you were anything but a dried-up weasel. Why, hell, you're damned near scared to death!"

"No more than you are, by God! And don't talk to me like that! If it wasn't for me, you and Hamaker would still be a couple of petty thieves waylaying travelers for what you could find in their pockets." He was turning as he spoke, his hand gripping the Derringer so tightly his knuckles were white.

He knew Bosma had seen him draw. Bosma was probably the fastest man he had ever seen. Unless he took Bosma by surprise the sheriff could put five shots into him while he was firing only one.

He thumbed back the hammer of the Derringer as he turned. From five feet away he exposed the gun and tightened his finger on the spur trigger.

A hard-pulling trigger, it always had been. In the instant while he put the necessary pressure on it, Bosma flung himself aside like a cat, drawing as he did.

Pettigrew fired, panic seizing him. The bullet missed, went past Bosma, and struck the window.

It shattered and shards of glass came *tinkling* to the floor and to the walk outside.

Bosma could have held his fire, knowing Pettigrew couldn't shoot again, but he did not. With deliberate viciousness, with regularly spaced meticulousness, he put five bullets into Pettigrew, three of them before he even struck the floor. Pain was brief and terrible for the judge and then there was no pain, no awareness, no light. There was nothing but darkness, eternal and complete.

Rufus came out of the swivel chair as though shot from a gun. He scrambled across the room toward Pettigrew, but stopped before he reached the man. He turned and stared dazedly at Bosma.

Bosma said: "The son-of-a-bitch is dead. Carry him back and put him in one of the cells. Put Dell's body with him. Then load up a shotgun and come with me."

XVIII

The shots Bosma fired earlier as he killed Dixon Fetters woke several of the men who had promised help to Sam Duke. They dressed hastily, snatched up their guns, and headed for the source of the commotion.

However, since the disturbance seemed in no way to threaten or involve Sam Duke, they retired after hastily discussing the matter, and returned to their homes without showing themselves or becoming part of it.

The second burst of shots, coming less than an hour after the others, found most of them still awake, fearful and worried, wondering if they had been wise in offering their help. Death could come to men very quickly in Los Finados if they dared miscalculate.

But at the second burst of shots they again dressed hastily, snatched up their guns again, and ran from their doors.

Les Neidrach met Mike Daley as he trotted toward the center of town and almost shot him before he realized who he was. They went on half a block and were joined by Jubal Jones, who lived closer than they to the center of the town. Neidrach panted softly: "Where'd those shots come from? Could you tell?"

"Lower end of town, I think. Near the sheriff's office."

They rounded the corner into the main street in time to see Bosma and Rufus coming out of the sheriff's office. Both men carried shotguns in addition to the revolvers at their sides.

Neidrach whispered: "Looks like this is it. Let's get on over to Duke's place."

They crossed the street hastily and paused in a dark doorway on the far side, waiting until they could go on without risking discovery by Bosma and Rufus, prepared to engage them if they came past.

But both men turned off before they reached the doorway and headed toward the other edge of town.

Neidrach whispered: "Maybe we've got enough time, after all. They've gone after Hamaker and some of his men."

The three emerged from the doorway and hurried on to Sam Duke's house.

He had also heard the shots. From the open doorway he called softly but distinctly: "Hold it right there. Just hold it where you are."

Neidrach called: "It's us, Neidrach and Daley and Jones! We just saw Bosma and Rufus heading toward Hamaker's place. The shots came from the sheriff's office, Jubal thinks."

"Come on in. Think anyone else is going to come?"

Neidrach said—"Sure. Sure they will."—but his voice was not as sure as his words.

They came into the house but Sam remained at the door, trying to penetrate the darkness with his eyes.

The showdown was here. Dawn was less than an hour away yet he seemed to sense that by dawn the thing would be over. He would be alive and the town would be rid of its oppressors, or he would be dead and things would remain unchanged. He wished briefly that he could see ahead, if only for an hour or two. The roar of a shotgun from the other side of town, repeated almost immediately by another gun, brought the worried comment from one of the men behind him in the room: "That would be the others, Les."

"They must've run into Bosma. I hope. . . ."

Sam said harshly: "I told you this wouldn't be cheap. I told you someone would get hurt. Maybe the others aren't going to come and maybe we'll all get killed. So make up your minds. Nobody is forcing you to stay."

Grace's voice interrupted instantly: "Sam! Are you trying to chase them away?"

Sam said: "I don't want men I can't count on."

He closed the door and stood facing them with his back against it. The blackness of night was now tempered slightly by a line of dark gray hanging like a cloud above the eastern horizon. Some of that cold, gray light seeped into the room—not enough to illuminate their faces or expressions, but only their shapes.

No one spoke and at last Sam said: "Well? I'm not going to talk to you again about what you're fighting. You know that better than I ever could. But I do want to know if you're going to fight?"

Neidrach cleared his throat. When he spoke, his voice was angry and loud. "We'll fight, by God, as long as you will."

"Daley?"

"We'll fight."

"Jones?"

"We're here, ain't we?"

"All right then. Neidrach, you stay with me. What kind of gun have you got?"

"Two. A rifle and a ten gauge."

"Plenty of powder?"

"Uhn-huh."

"How about you two?"

Daley said: "Got my revolver and carbine."

"Jones?"

"Shotgun. Buckshot and plenty of powder."

Sam asked: "Grace, can you load a gun?"

"I think so, Sam."

Sam said: "All of you put your powder and shot on the table. Grace will load, but she'll probably need some help. Load your own if she's busy. And, Grace, keep low. On the floor if you can."

He swung back toward the door, opened it slightly, and stared outside. He spoke softly over his shoulder. "Jones, you and Daley watch the back of the house. Move around from window to window. It'll make them think we've got more men than we have." He heard them moving away. He heard Grace and Neidrach talking softly at the table as he showed her how to load. He said: "This will play hell with your house."

She got no chance to reply, for immediately on the heels of his words a harsh shout raised outside: "Come on out Duke! We've got men all around the place. Come out and meet me face to face. If you kill me, you can walk out of town a free man."

Sam waited an instant, then yelled: "Bosma?"

"Yeah?"

"Hamaker there, too? And Pettigrew?"

"Pettigrew's dead. Hamaker's here."

"Then I'll tell you. That last wagon train . . . it was mine. One of the men you killed was my brother. So you understand what I'm doing here. I came to kill you . . . all four of you. I'll get you two, at least."

He caught a flash of movement across the street and fired instantly. He heard a howl, saw another flurry of movement that immediately disappeared.

His shot was answered by a volley resembling a string of firecrackers exploding all at once. Bullets *thudded* into the front wall of the house, shattering a window, showering Sam with splinters. A pellet from a shotgun struck him in the thigh, stinging, burning, probably imbedding itself.

He ducked behind the door. Neidrach flopped to the floor and so did Grace. If there were only a little more light. . . .

He wished he could expect more men but he knew that he could not. Judging from the shots they had heard, Bosma had, he thought, caught someone heading here and killed him. That had been enough to discourage others with the same idea.

He eased the door open slightly and peered outside again. The light didn't seem to have increased at all. Gun flashes blossomed spasmodically across the street, and bullets occasionally struck the house.

Sam realized with a sinking, hopeless feeling that unless something happened to change the present situation, they were doomed. They couldn't hope to win out against such superior odds. Bosma must have fifteen men out there. They could keep the defenders down by spasmodic sniping and under its cover slip in close without being seen. They could fire the house or burst inside and overwhelm the occupants.

Sam scowled. Was all the planning, all the anger and outrage and determination to come to this? Were they going to die here in this house, their purpose forgotten with their deaths?

He heard Jones and Daley open up from the rear of the house. He left the door and hurried to the kitchen. Daley turned his head and said: "We drove 'em into that stable back there. There ain't cover out here like there is in front . . . only the stable and the high weeds in back of it."

Sam's eyes brightened. He asked: "How many? Could you tell?"

"Must've been ten of 'em or more. Maybe they was planning to rush the house. Maybe they didn't figure we could see 'em as well as we could."

Gun flashes began to show in the doors and windows of the stable. A bullet came through one of the kitchen windows—high—shattering the glass and bringing pieces of it *tinkling* to the floor, showering Daley as they came. He swiped at his bleeding face and cursed.

Sam said: "I'm going to flush 'em out of there. Don't waste ammunition shooting at the shed. But when they come out, shoot carefully and shoot to kill. Understand?"

"You can't flush 'em out."

"I think I can." He turned his head to yell at Neidrach: "Keep 'em busy out front!"

Neidrach didn't answer. His gun answered for him as he fired at half seen targets across the street in the dark gray light of dawn.

Daylight, Sam knew, would favor neither side.

He started out the back door, heard Grace's soft: "Sam. No."

He said harshly—"Keep on loading."—and went on out, running as he cleared the back door, weaving and dodging, making an elusive target for the guns in the door and windows of the stable.

Daley and Jones held their fire, waiting, as they had been instructed. Sam felt the twitch of a bullet tearing through the leg of his pants, scratching his leg as it passed. He heard the roar of a shotgun and felt the veritable shower of birdshot raining against his back, stinging, feeling like a thousand red-hot coals. If that had been buckshot instead of birdshot. . . .

He hit the ground, rolling, came to his feet, and zigzagged away. Two men left the shed in pursuit and now Jones's and Daley's guns opened up from the house. Both men fell and lay kicking, twitching on the ground.

Those remaining in the stable switched their attention from Sam to the pair in the house. He disappeared into the dark, gray dawn.

The town remained dark, but Sam knew every inhabitant was awake. Awake and waiting nervously for the outcome. He might not have their physical support but he knew they were on his side and even that helped right now.

Safe from the guns in the stable, he circled rapidly, running, his breathing ragged and hoarse. There was not much time. In seconds he would be too late. The situation would change. Those in the stable would leave it in pursuit of him, keeping Jones and Daley pinned down with a barrage laid down by one or two of their number.

He reached the high, dry weeds behind the shed. Scarcely slowing his pace, he gathered up a double armload of them and deposited them against the dry frame wall of the shed. Crouching, he struck a match and dropped it into the center of the pile.

Light grew rapidly, *crackling,* spreading. Sam got up and sprinted away, to flop in safety a hundred yards away.

The thing was done, he thought triumphantly. The battle wasn't won but the tide was turned. The men in the stable would have to leave, for it would catch and burn to the ground. Leaving, they would make perfect targets silhouetted against the fire's light.

He wondered where Bosma and Hamaker were. Not in the shed, he was willing to bet. They were across the street, behind a tree or house. They were directing the battle but not fighting it.

The fire grew rapidly, spreading through the high, dry weeds until it covered a spot larger than the stable itself. Flames began to lick up the rear stable wall, catching in the dry, warped walls. Soon now, he thought. Soon the occupants of the stable would come running out. He hoped fervently that both Jones and Daley were good shots.

He got his own spare revolver cylinder out of his pocket and held it in his left hand, the gun itself in his right. He didn't know how many shots he had left in the gun, but he knew he could change in seconds when he did run out.

Some place beyond the house he heard Bosma's shouting voice but he could not make out the words. Then the first man left the shed, bending low, running as though the devil were in pursuit.

Sam rested his revolver on his knee, sighted carefully, pulled ahead slightly to lead the man, and fired. A shotgun bellowed simultaneously from the house.

The man pitched forward and lay, spread-eagled, on the ground, still and dead. Another burst from the stable, half turned, firing at the house as he ran. Sam fired again but this time the hammer fell on an empty chamber.

Not so the house. The shotgun roared and the man doubled as though the charge had taken him in the belly. He, too, lay still.

They burst away in a group, then, three turning one way, three another. But Sam had his spare cylinder in. He fired at the lead man on the right, missed, fired again. The man went down. The second man on the right also went down, his leg cut out from under him by a shot from the house. He crawled crabwise toward the concealment of darkness beyond the reach of the fire's light.

The third man got away, as did the first man on

the left. Sam's gun swung and took the second. A rifle from the house caught the last one and drove him, stumbling, half running and off balance, toward the safety of unburned weeds beyond the fire's reach.

Sam got up and ran recklessly for the house. The others would be coming from across the street. If he was caught out here. . . .

He saw them coming as he rounded the stable, running toward him from both sides of the house. He fired once, then hit the door bodily, and burst through, rolling, smashing a table and chair as he tumbled across the room.

He was up instantly. Daley lay prone beside one of the windows. Jones stood ready, waiting for a target, at the other.

Sam stepped over Daley and stared outside. A bullet struck the window frame and showered him with splinters and chips of paint. But there were no targets at which to shoot. A glance at the corpse-littered ground had been enough for Hamaker's men. The yard outside was still as death.

Grace came running into the kitchen. She gave Sam one terrified look, one quick glance that held a world of relief that he was safe, then turned her attention to Mike Daley, kneeling beside him on the floor. When she rose, there was shock in her face, a terrible numbness and stunned disbelief. She said softly: "Sam. Oh, Sam, he's dead."

A burst of shots racketed, dim with distance, between them and the business section of the town. Sam put his arms around Grace and held her close with her face buried against his chest. He said: "They're running and I'm not going to let them go. Stay here with Neidrach and Jones."

She opened her mouth to protest but remained silent when she saw the direction of his glance, resting on the body of Daley beneath the shattered window. He pulled away and went quickly through the house. Bosma and Hamaker would run and so would as many of Hamaker's men as were still alive and able to ride. And the town would probably let them go rather than risk engaging them again.

But Sam wouldn't. He had ridden here for vengeance and would not ride away without finding it.

XIX

A strange feeling possessed Sam Duke as he left the house—the feeling that this night had been composed, not of hours but of days. Dawn seemed to be taking forever to come. Its first gray had been showing in the east as Bosma and Hamaker attacked the house, and it was scarcely lighter now. The battle had been violent, but fast and soon over.

He needn't worry about Grace. Neidrach and Jones would take care of her, guard her against any of Hamaker's men who might be wounded and dangerous. Apparently those yet unhurt had lost their courage after seeing the heavy toll taken of those trying to escape the burning stable. They'd scatter like quail and he'd never get them all. But he could get Bosma and Hamaker. He would follow those two, if necessary, until he did.

He walked toward the center of town quickly but warily, gun in hand, all too conscious that there were only three loads left in it, knowing he didn't dare return to the house and take time to reload. Neither Bosma nor Hamaker would stay in town any longer than was necessary to get their money and a horse. Neither would now have the courage to face both Sam and an aroused and hostile town.

The sky grew lighter as he walked. Behind him,

the burning stable sent up a thick black pillar of smoke. Already some of the townspeople were running toward it, carrying buckets and other containers. Sam passed several of them on the street but apparently their fear of Bosma and Hamaker was still strong enough to keep them from offering to help.

And Sam didn't want their help. Not now. He may have caused the deaths of both Fetters and Pettigrew, but he could not help feeling cheated of that part of his vengeance. He wouldn't be cheated of this. Bosma and Hamaker were the worst, Hamaker because he had led the murderous gang attacking the wagon trains, Bosma because by callous brutality and viciousness he had kept the town in line.

He entered the main street and stopped. With careful eyes that missed nothing, he studied the length of it. Except for a single, small tan dog crossing diagonally toward the hotel, it was deserted. The dog sat down in the middle of the dusty street and scratched. Then he got up, wandered up onto the hotel verandah, and laid down, facing the street. He panted lightly, his tongue hanging out.

A fierce exultation touched Sam as he saw Bosma come from behind the sheriff's office, leading a horse. Hamaker was nowhere in sight.

Hamaker could be concealed on any roof, in any window, between any two buildings between here and the jail. He could be waiting, rifle in hand, for Sam to come within easy range.

Some of Hamaker's men might be with him or might be similarly concealed. The street might be an elaborately baited trap, with Bosma and his led horse down at the far end of it being the irrefutable bait.

Sam thought briefly and with regret of Grace, of the promise she had held out to him. He realized that his chances of ever seeing her again were very poor. He must walk down this street openly, knowing it was a trap and trusting his senses alone to warn him before he was cut down from ambush by Hamaker or one of his men.

There was another way, but it was unpalatable to him. He could let Bosma and Hamaker go. Then he could organize a posse of the townspeople and take up the pursuit. A surer method, he supposed. A safer one. But a solution that would neither please Sam nor erase the memory of his brother and their teamsters lying scattered and crumpled in the dry dust where their camp had been.

Bosma tied the horse in front of the jail and turned to face Sam. There was insolence in his stance, plainly visible even though the distance between them was more than two hundred yards.

Sam began to walk toward him, his steps steady, measured, tense. At any instant a rifle might shout at him from either side or from behind. A shotgun might spray him with lethal pellets. If that happened, Bosma would ride insolently away, winner in the end. An intolerable thought. He would crawl, if he must, the two hundred yards that separated them. He would live long enough to put a bullet squarely in the center of Bosma's gloating face.

He avoided glancing visibly to right or left, but his eyes were busy nevertheless and alert for the slightest movement at the edge of his vision range.

At a hundred yards, he halted as Bosma yelled: "It's you and me, Duke! Just you and me. Where do you want me to bury you? Down there where your wagons are or where you buried your brother and teamsters?"

Taunting. For a purpose. Taunting to make Sam reckless and careless of whoever might be waiting to ambush him from behind while Bosma held his attention to the front. But taunting that achieved, at least, a part of its purpose. It raised the angry pressure inside Sam's head. It made his eyes burn with fury. It made recklessness rise in him like a fire in dry grass.

There was a way—there had to be a way of reaching Bosma without being murdered from behind.

He scowled. If he continued this measured pacing down the street toward the jail where Bosma waited for him, he'd just never get there.

He'd make a relatively easy target for Hamaker and whoever else was waiting for him to pass.

But if he ran—a moving target is not so easy to hit. If he ducked and dodged down that street like a fleeing deer in high brush, there might be a chance of reaching the jail without being too badly hit to finish the job when he arrived.

Too little time remained for the decision he must make. At any instant Hamaker's gun might bawl, and either a rifle ball or a load of buckshot would come whistling toward him.

He took a sudden step to the right, then lunged forward in a run. Instantly, like an echo to his movement, a gun roared less than fifty feet behind and to the right of him. He heard the pellets of buckshot like a sudden, high gust of wind passing by his head. He heard them strike the street and from a corner of his eye saw the dozen or more separate clouds of dust they raised.

He was moving now, moving, but he would have hoped Hamaker had a rifle instead of that damned shotgun loaded with buckshot. He would have hoped to be farther away before Hamaker cut loose.

Forget Bosma for a moment and concentrate on Hamaker instead. A running target at fifty feet is fairly difficult to hit with a rifle, easy with a scatter-gun.

He dived to the ground, rolling, concentrating all his attention on the spot back of him from which that first blast had come. As he rolled, raising a dry cloud of dust, he caught a glimpse of Hamaker, gun to his shoulder. The twin bores looked as large as those of a cannon.

He made one complete, rolling turn before he glimpsed Hamaker again and could bring his gun to bear. More than ever before, in this lightning instant, he was conscious of the fact that in the split second while he fired he would be motionless, a sitting duck for Hamaker and his scatter-gun.

His gun centered and bucked ferociously in his hand. Like an echo the shotgun roared and the lethal dose of buckshot was on its way.

Frozen, immobile, he stared at Hamaker. It was an instant before he comprehended the little puff of dust that came from Hamaker's chest. But the effect of the bullet's impact was plainer and more quickly understood. The man drove back ponderously, his legs failing to keep pace. The muzzle of the shotgun raised.

Shot whistled close over Sam Duke's head. But not all of them. He felt one tear into his shoulder muscles, another take him in the thigh. Striking him, they burned as though red hot and pain spread from the area until his whole arm and leg felt numb.

Now Hamaker was down. The empty shotgun *clattered* harmlessly at his side. He didn't move.

Sam struggled to his feet. Bosma had whirled

and started to untie his horse. But a dozen towns-men suddenly appeared behind him, all armed, all determined, all silently warning him not to try escape.

Limping, Sam slowly covered the remaining distance separating him from the murderous sheriff. The ball was in his right shoulder and could stiffen it. He only had two shots, having used one on Hamaker.

He said harshly: "End of the road, Bosma. Pay day. Even if you kill me, do you think they'll let you go? You're going to die, Bosma, and find out what it was like for all the ones you killed."

Bosma's head yanked around. He stared at the silent, menacing group between himself and the limits of the town. When he again looked at Sam, the contemplation of death was in his eyes, perhaps for the first time in his whole, vicious life. He was in a game he couldn't win no matter what he did.

He said with quick softness: "I'll make a deal with you. You can have the money . . . all of it . . . over fifteen thousand dollars. And both of us can live."

This was the satisfaction Sam had wanted—the satisfaction of having Bosma break, but it sickened him all the same. He said: "There's only one way this can end . . . with you dead. I promised my brother that, and I promised myself. Get your gun out, Bosma, and get it over with."

An instant more, an instant while panic and terror firmed in Bosma's eyes to determination and fatalistic acceptance.

The man's hand was like light as it streaked down toward his gun in the fastest draw Sam Duke had ever seen. He knew he was closer to death than he had ever been before.

But his own action was as reflexive as Bosma's. His gun was in his hand, raising, the hammer back and the barrel falling into line before his mind had time to will his body to react. The gun slammed against his palm and flame and smoke shot from the muzzle of it.

Bosma's bullet burned along his ribs and then his own heavy slug tore into Bosma's throat. Blood shot from the wound like a fountain. Bosma staggered forward, choking, to collapse into a heap on the ground. The blood streaming from his throat was briefly red before it was absorbed by the deep, dry dust. He choked noisily for several moments, and then was still.

Sam stared on down the street at the townspeople who had blocked Bosma's escape from town. He holstered his gun and turned.

He saw her coming toward him, running, and knew that she had watched it all. He saw the rifle in her hands that she would have used if he had been killed. It dropped when she realized she was carrying it.

There was a woman, he thought, who would

stand by his side for as long as he lived, a part of him like his own right hand. There was a woman, all woman, who could give life a meaning he had never known it could possess.

His wounds forgotten, he strode to meet her, a smile beginning to grow on his long, strong mouth. He had lost much, but he had found much, too. Grace was his. He was alive. And the morning sun was on his back, warm and good.

About the Author

Lewis B. Patten wrote more than ninety Western novels in thirty years, and three of them won Spur Awards from the Western Writers of America, and the author received the Golden Saddleman Award. Indeed, this points up the most remarkable aspect of his work: not that there is so much of it, but that so much of it is so fine. Patten was born in Denver, Colorado, and served in the U.S. Navy, 1933–1937. He was educated at the University of Denver during the war years and became an auditor for the Colorado Department of Revenue during the 1940s. It was in this period that he began contributing significantly to Western pulp magazines, fiction that was from the beginning fresh and unique and revealed Patten's lifelong concern with the sociological and psychological affects of group psychology on the frontier. He became a professional writer at the time of his first novel, *Massacre at White River* (1952). The dominant theme in much of his fiction is the notion of justice, and its opposite, injustice. In his first novel it has to do with exploitation of the Ute Indians, but as he matured as a writer he explored this theme with significant and poignant detail in small towns throughout the early West. Crimes, such as rape or lynching, are often at the center of his stories. When the values embodied in these small towns are examined closely, they are found to be wanting. Conformity is always easier than taking a stand. Yet, in Patten's view of the American West, there is usually a man or a woman who refuses to conform. Among his finest titles, always a difficult choice, are surely *Death of a Gunfighter* (1968), *A Death in Indian Wells* (1970), and *The Law at Cottonwood* (1978). No less noteworthy are his previous Five Star Westerns, *Tincup in the Storm Country*, *Trail to Vicksburg*, *Death Rides the Denver Stage*, *The Woman at Ox-Yoke*, and *Ride the Red Trail*.

Additional Copyright Information

Center Point Large Print
600 Brooks Road / PO Box 1
Thorndike ME 04986-0001 USA

(207) 568-3717

US & Canada:
1 800 929-9108
www.centerpointlargeprint.com